A CHANGE IN PERSPECTIVE

A GRANITE COVE NOVEL

DENISE CARBO

Editing: Nancy Haight, EditorNancy.com

❀ Created with Vellum

For my grandmother: Ruth. We lost her young, but I will always treasure the memories of Christmas on the farm in Wolfeboro.

PROLOGUE

*I*s it possible to have a nervous breakdown at twenty-seven?
There's a roaring in my ears, as if I'm trapped in a tunnel underneath the ocean with water pouring in through a gaping trench, and it's barreling toward me like a freight train.

My jaw aches from clenching my teeth together, or it's because I constantly grind my teeth. I still haven't followed my dentist's advice to wear a mouth guard at night or to alleviate the stress in my life.

It could ache from the screaming fit I just had at the office. My throat is certainly raw.

You would think a partner in a law firm would have enough sense not to pat the ass of one of their female lawyers. Did he really believe I would welcome the attention? Did he think I would smile politely and let him grope me?

My chest feels like there's a vacuum attached to my lungs and it's sucking all the air out.

I quit my job!

I suppose the proper thing to do would've been to quietly report him to the human resources department—which I did, belatedly. Throwing his stupid golf award into his computer screen and threatening to sue him into oblivion if he ever touched me again might have been over the top.

And now the two cars blocking my entrance into my garage haven't magically disappeared. I drum my fingers on the top of my steering wheel. Why didn't Mark drive his car, or the white convertible sitting next to it, into the garage?

No, they left both cars out in the driveway for all the neighbors to see.

I guess I can't keep pretending I don't know he's cheating on me.

Three days of telling myself I was paranoid.

Three days of denial.

Whoever she is, she left lipstick on the neckline of one of my dresses. It hung by itself with the clothes on either side pushed aside. The dress was hard to miss in my orderly closet. The glossy, red shade of lipstick stood out like a beacon on the white dress. I'd never wear that shade of red. It would clash with my coloring.

She wanted me to see. It's the only explanation.

I climb out of my car and stroll up the brick pathway we had installed two months ago. Had he been screwing her then?

They left the front door unlocked. Giggling drifts down the stairs.

There's an iceberg floating in my stomach, and it's spreading a frozen chill throughout my body. My fingers twitch at my sides. I flick the tips of my lavender nails, making them click.

Modern furniture fills the open floor plan. Mark's mother gifted us her design skills as a housewarming gift. The cement dining room table probably weighs as much as my car. The animal print rug lies in the center of the living room like a ritualistic sacrifice. The gray couch is so uncomfortable no one sits on it for more than a few minutes. I hate every inch of this place.

I stride over to the mantel and snatch the glass sculpture I purchased on our honeymoon in Venice. It's solid and heavy. I clutch it to my chest and climb the stairs.

The bed creaking and the slap of skin sliding together grows louder. They left the door open. I wrinkle my nose over the smell of sex and sweat filling the room.

She's skinnier than me—a lot skinnier. She barely has any curves. Her hair is dark brown to my blonde. She's older too. She has to be at least thirty-five. What does he see in her? What didn't I provide?

I clutch the sculpture tighter between my breasts.

They're too enraptured with each other to even see me standing in the open doorway.

I bet I could walk right up to the bed. My bed.

My bedroom.

My house.

My husband.

I stroke a finger down the smooth side of the glass. It's heavy enough to do considerable damage. One well-aimed hit would cause tremendous pain and probably a concussion.

Two or three hits in quick succession could incapacitate both of them. Perhaps it would do much worse.

Am I capable of that?

Isn't anyone under the right circumstances? When they've been pushed too far and can't stand a minute more?

I could plea temporary insanity. I'm sure there are precedents to site.

I might even get away with it. At worst, a plea bargain and a few years of good behavior might have me out on parole before I'm too old to start over.

The blue and green threads twist and entwine inside the glass. Red would clash with the sensual beauty of the sculpture. Mark and his whores aren't worth another ounce of my life.

"Is this the one who's been trying on my clothes and leaving lipstick on them, or is this another one?" I stride across the room to my closet. "I suggest you hire a divorce lawyer."

The woman shrieks as Mark shoves her to the floor and scrambles out of the bed.

I grab my suitcases and stuff the sculpture into one. Handfuls of clothes follow as I snatch them off hangers and shelves.

Mark ushers the woman out of the bedroom with her clothes hanging in her arms despite her vociferous protests.

I fill a second suitcase and open a third.

He appears in the open doorway while yanking on a pair of pants. "Baby, I know you're upset. Let's talk about this."

"You can have the house. Buy me out."

He grabs my arm. "Baby—"

I yank my arm free and stalk into the bathroom. One by one, I rip out the drawers and upend the contents into my bag.

"It won't happen again. It's just sex. It means nothing."

"That's what you said last time."

CHAPTER 1

ranny slaps Olivia on the arm. "Tell me that is some horrible illusion, and your brother did not just walk by with Vanessa hanging on his arm."

Olivia rubs her arm and cranes her neck to peer out the window of the bakery. "I hate to disappoint you, but she's Ollie's realtor. As far as I know that's all it is, but with my brother, you never know."

I peek around Franny. Oliver's tall form is easy to spot, and so is the dark-headed woman strolling next to him in a short black skirt and three-inch heels. Her legs must be freezing. The damp April weather hovers around forty degrees. I shiver in my sweater and leggings just thinking about strolling down the sidewalk with my thighs exposed.

"Luce, didn't you once say you wanted Oliver to be your rebound guy? You should go say hello and save him from her before he makes a horrible mistake. He might end up like one of those doomed characters in one of Luke's novels." Franny waves her finger between Olivia and me. "You know the one I'm talking about. The wife kept her husband chained in her attic for years when he threatened to leave her. She told everyone he was dead."

Olivia's mouth drops open and she stares out the window. "I love my husband's books, but I don't want my brother dating anyone who resembles one of his characters—especially not that one."

I pat my sister's hand. "Franny, I say this with love. You're sounding a little crazy. Vanessa isn't the spawn of Satan."

It's been two years since I left Mark. Oliver is a very handsome man. I've jokingly mentioned I wouldn't mind him being my first foray back into dating. But that was before he decided to move back to town. He seemed like a safer choice then. I wouldn't have to see him if our date went horribly wrong. Now, I'd probably run into him too often.

Franny's twisted her apron strings around her fingers like a tourniquet. "You better let go of the apron before you cut off the circulation in your fingers. You won't be able to bake for the rest of the day, and didn't you say you had a specialty cake you needed to finish?"

She frees her fingers and pushes the apron across the table. "She may not be the devil's spawn, but she's definitely on his invite list."

"Well shoot, now I feel like I should go save my brother from her evil clutches. Lucinda, are you sure you're no longer interested?"

I smile at Olivia and take a sip of my tea. A hint of lemon bursts over my tongue. "I didn't say that..."

"I'll call Mitch. We'll have a little get-together at our house." Franny points to Olivia. "You and Luke." She nods at me. "And you and Oliver."

"Real subtle, Franny. I think I'd prefer something a little less blatant. That sounds as bad as a blind date." I tap my fingers against the black iron table. The heavenly smell of baked goods wafts through the small dining space. I glance over my shoulder.

Sally drops two everything bagels into the bakery's black bag with pink writing and hands it to a customer.

Franny waves her hand dismissively. "It's not a blind date. You've already met a couple of times."

Olivia laughs. "I think you're missing the point, Franny. Lucinda is right. Oliver has never been one to let me set him up with anyone, and he would see that as a total set up. He'd probably bail on the whole thing. I'd also have to tell him there's no longer a ban on him dating any of my friends."

"There's a ban?"

She rolls her eyes. "Oh yes. I had to start the ban in high school. He dated one of my best friends, and after they were through, she barely ever spoke to me again."

"Ouch." I frown. "He broke her heart?"

Olivia winces. "I told you he's a player. He never gets serious. Women always think he will, though. You'd have to be sure you're only looking for a short fling with him and nothing long-term or monogamous."

"Honestly, I'm not sure if I'm ready for even that. I haven't been with anyone since the divorce, not even a date. It's been two years. Is it weird I don't know if I'm ready to date yet? It's not like I have any residual feelings for Mark or anything. Those died a long time ago, even before the divorce." I shrug. "I guess I just don't have the interest in all the drama of dating, or even a fling with no strings attached."

Franny squeezes my hand. "Luce, don't let my emotional outburst push you into doing anything you're not absolutely ready for. Obviously, I still have unresolved issues where Vanessa is concerned. It's hard to forget all the years she bullied me. You'll date when you're ready."

"As a divorcee myself, I don't think there's a set time limit after a divorce for when you should start dating. Everyone is different. It took quite a while for me, too." Olivia sends me a comforting smile from across the table.

7

I bump Franny's shoulder with mine. "Look on the bright side, Oliver might break Vanessa's heart. She deserves a heck of a lot of bad karma."

Franny chuckles. "I didn't think of it that way. You're right."

"I'm not sure I like the image of my brother as a karmic weapon, but if anyone could do it, it would probably be Ollie."

Franny stands and pushes the long sleeves of her green top up. "On that note, I better get back to work. The cake isn't going to decorate itself."

"Break time is over." Olivia stands too. "I've got to get those new pictures uploaded to the bakery website."

"I'm going to finish my tea before I head upstairs to my apartment." I lift it slightly in the air as they scoot past me. I have a lengthy list of calls to make today and a meeting with a potential client this afternoon. There's a momentary pang as Franny and Olivia disappear behind the bakery counter. I miss helping out in the bakery and chatting with them on a regular basis. We'll have to make these breaktime visits a weekly occurrence.

Thanks to Franny and Mitch's wedding and, more recently Kelly and Holden's, my wedding planning business has a decent number of clients. Celebrity weddings can't be beat for advertising, but people quickly forget too. I need to build a solid local base, which means I need to stop working out of my apartment and find a professional workspace.

It's a bit of a catch twenty-two. I need the space to keep the clients coming, but I need the clients to pay for the space. Renting a storefront in the village isn't exactly cheap. Granite Cove's prime real estate is the village because of the lakefront and the charming historical buildings lining Main Street. I'll have to find an office on the newer side of town, and I won't be asking Vanessa to be my real estate agent.

I really need to come up with fresh ideas for wedding venues to offer my clients, too. Unique destinations, as well as a wide range of suggestions, should entice prospective brides. The wedding venues in the area aren't extensive. White Birch Inn hosts small weddings, and I've left them my card, but they usually handle their events in-house. The country club has the largest space, and thanks to my parents being longtime members, they've agreed to send interested parties my way.

Rebecca's intimate beach wedding was beautiful, but on a private beach. I should make a list of public beaches and see if we need a permit. Franny's wedding was on their private estate. The inn is the closest offering for a lakeside wedding. There might be private owners willing to rent space for events.

I finish my tea, chuck the cup into the trash receptacle, and slip behind the counter. Olivia has come back up front and is helping Sally with the customers. I didn't even notice the sudden surge of customers while I was finishing my tea. I try to catch her eye to wave goodbye, but she's smiling and chatting with Bobby Calvert.

His blond hair curls over his ears. He's already sporting a bit of a tan even though it's only early spring. He grins at something Olivia says. *So he is capable of being friendly.* Every time I've waited on him when I've filled in at the bakery, he's barely said two words.

Although, he usually comes in earlier in the morning. Not everyone is a morning person. I should give him the benefit of the doubt.

I walk over and stand next to Olivia and face Bobby. "Hi Bobby. Picking up some raspberry turnovers?" I remember they're his favorite.

His smile vanishes. "Thanks, Olivia." Bobby turns and walks out of the bakery without acknowledging me at all.

Okay, not the time of day. It must be me he doesn't like.

Olivia leans close. "Is there some history there I'm not aware of?"

I glance at her and force a smile. "If there is, I'm in the dark. I mean, we went to high school together."

"Maybe it was just my imagination, but he seemed to get a little frosty toward you."

"Not your imagination. He's always that way with me, and I don't understand why."

"Strange. You never dated him or anything? Did he ask you out and you turned him down?"

"No. He dated one of my closest friends for a while." I shrug. "I'm going to head through the kitchen and say goodbye to Franny. I'll see you later."

"Bye."

Franny stands in front of a several-tier high white cake with pink flowers cascading down the side. She adds a ribbon of pale pink along the top edge of the bottom tier. The sweet scent of frosting tickles my nose as I walk past.

"I won't disturb you. I'm on my way up to my apartment." I point to the stairs outside her back door.

"Okay." She raises her head. "Hey, did you read this month's book for book club yet?"

I stop at the long marble counter in the center of the room. "Not yet, why?"

"My copy is in my tote." She tilts her head toward the hooks on the wall. Her black canvas tote with The Sweet Spot logo hangs on one of the hooks. "You can read mine. I already finished it."

"Thanks." I pluck the book out of her tote. The cover has a dragon on the front. "Is it any good?"

She nods. "I stayed up way past my bedtime the other night. Gets pretty steamy too."

"I could use some steamy." My lady parts seemed to have gone into hibernation. I open the door. "Bye. Love you."

"Love you too."

I close the door and gaze at the lake spread out before me.

Franny's bakery has a prime spot. Even though the sky is overcast and gray, a few boats are in the cove and farther out. I glance over at the marina on the other side of the parking lot behind the stores lining Main Street. Boats already fill half the marina. Over the next few weeks, it will fill to capacity as people put their boats in the water for the season. A chilly breeze whips my hair over my face and sends an icy tingle down my back. I should've grabbed my coat instead of dashing down the stairs in nothing but a sweater. I push my hair off my face.

Bobby stands next to his truck with Calvert Landscaping on the door. He's chatting with an older gentleman I don't recognize.

Why doesn't he like me?

He and Jackie dated for most of our junior year. We never really went on a double date or anything, but I don't remember her saying he had a problem with me. Although, I don't remember him being at a lot of the school functions either.

The man he was talking to walks away with a wave. Bobby waves back and stares out at the lake.

I'll never learn why if I don't ask.

I stride across the alleyway between the bakery and Skis 'n' Things into the parking lot. He opens his door.

"Bobby!"

His blond head turns and his gaze finds me. He frowns and folds his arms over his chest.

At least he didn't ignore me and drive away.

I stop next to him and flash him my sunniest smile. His frown doesn't ease.

"Have I done something to offend you? I get the impression you don't like me much."

"What, you can't stand the thought that not everyone is a member of your fan club?"

I rear my head back. His animosity is definitely not my imagination.

"Of course not, but I want to know if I've offended you in some way. If you just don't like me, then fine."

"I just don't like you." He climbs into his truck and drives away while I stand there trying not to let my mouth hang open.

I clear my suddenly dry throat and glance around to see if anyone witnessed my humiliation. Thankfully, no one in the area appears to be paying me any attention. Of course, they could be avoiding eye contact.

It's my own fault. I just had to know what the problem was. Is he right? Can I not stand it if someone doesn't like me?

I shuffle back to the steps of my apartment. Is it wrong to want people to like me? Who doesn't want people to like them?

CHAPTER 2

*a*n array of colors fill the various bouquets of flowers. Maybe I should buy one. It might cheer me up. It's not as if anyone is going to buy me flowers. The heavy floral scent from the wall of bouquets pervades the flower shop. I glance over at the potted plants on the tiered tables in the center of the space. Plants would be more economical and add some life to my apartment. It could be a test run. If I can keep a plant alive, I could move on to a pet.

I straighten my cream-colored stack of business cards on the counter of Blossoms. I'll have to order more cards soon. Should I keep them the same or go with a more economical version?

Rebecca taps me on the shoulder as she walks behind me and back around the counter. "I've been handing them out like hotcakes lately. Your business must be booming."

"It's been on a steady climb. I can't thank you enough for being so supportive and letting me put my cards here." My first year as a wedding planner is almost to the halfway point, and so far, I'm in the black, and I'm building up my savings to rent a place for business. It's not the total failure my mother predicted.

"Are you kidding? It's the very least I could do after you

threw together my impromptu wedding and refused to take a dime."

"It wasn't my business yet then, just a hobby of sorts. I promise to charge you if you and Ian decide to get married again—to each other, of course."

Rebecca laughs. "Once was enough. It was perfect. You've got a gift. You perceive exactly what the bride and groom want, even when they don't realize it themselves. I think I can speak for Franny, Olivia, and Kelly as well. Our weddings were perfect for each of us because you made them that way."

I reach over and squeeze Rebecca's hand. "Thanks, I needed to hear that today. I seem to question everything lately. Like these cards." I point to my business cards. Maybe the thick card stock with the gold intertwined wedding rings and lettering is too simple. They stand out nicely against her blue and silver theming, but they'd probably disappear against a plain back-ground. "Should I have them redone with some color? And opt for a thinner, less expensive card stock?"

Rebecca picks one up and examines it. "I don't think so. It screams classy and elegant to me."

"Hmm...I don't want people to think I only do expensive weddings, though."

"Which is why I think your slogan, 'Let me plan your dream wedding,' and the words, 'intimate to extravagant' underneath, are perfect. Why do you think you're questioning everything?"

I roll my eyes. "I seem to be on an introspection kick, or something. Maybe it's the divorce, the new career, or because I'll be turning thirty this year. I don't know."

"I think any of those could trigger an introspection period."

"Did you go through one when you turned thirty, moved here, or opened the flower shop?"

"Oh, I questioned the decision to move to Granite Cove and start a new business a few dozen times. Mostly, I was worried about Drew and if I was doing the right thing for him. Turning thirty wasn't really a big deal to me. I was too worried about other things."

Rebecca moved and started a new business all while taking care of her special needs brother. She made it look so easy. Why am I struggling? I glance behind me to make sure the shop is still empty and I'm not keeping Rebecca from her customers. "Would you describe me as a people pleaser and wanting everyone to like me?"

She tilts her head and studies me for a few seconds.

I should've kept my mouth shut.

"I think they can be two different things, and I don't believe either is all bad or all good. Nothing really is, is it?"

"What do you mean?"

"I'm more concerned with why you're asking, rather than if you have those traits. Did someone say something to you?"

I wave my hand dismissively. "It's not important. Like I said, I've just been questioning everything lately."

Rebecca grabs my hand. "Lucinda, I think you try very hard to always put on a brave, positive front for everyone. I rarely see you without a smile on your face. There's absolutely nothing wrong with that unless you're burying and hiding your pain behind that smile. No one expects you to be happy all the time. There's also nothing wrong with telling people no from time to time when you want to."

"So you *do* think I'm a people pleaser."

"Again, I don't think it's black and white. I think the more important question is if you think you are. From past conversations, I've concluded both you and Franny developed coping methods to deal with your overbearing mother. I also know you've stood up to her for Franny's sake and for your own when you moved back here and started a new career. And let's not forget you left your cheating husband and divorced his deluded, promiscuous, lying ass."

My lips twitch. "It wasn't the first time he cheated, though. I did stay."

Rebecca shrugs. "That's because you're a good person and think other people are too and believe they can change. I have less faith in humanity." She squeezes my hand and lets go as the door opens behind me. "Wanting people to like you isn't a bad thing either unless you're hurting yourself to get them to like you."

"Thanks, Rebecca. I can always count on you for honest advice. You don't sugarcoat it too much to spare my feelings."

"If you want blunt, I'm your gal. Just remember, don't go questioning yourself because of what anyone else does or says about you. They all have their own motives and perspectives. Only you can know your own truth."

She walks around the counter and goes to greet the customer while I leave.

Why did I stay with Mark after the first time he cheated? I don't think my reasons were as altruistic as Rebecca said. I wanted to believe he'd change, but deep down, I knew he wouldn't. I stayed because I was afraid to leave. Afraid to fail.

"Lucinda?"

I swivel on the sidewalk and gaze behind me. A familiar round face with ice-blue eyes smiles back at me. "Jackie?"

She closes the distance between us at a jog. Her knee-high boots click along the sidewalk and her leather tote bag bops against her jean clad thigh. Her black, curly hair is longer than I remember and streaked with red highlights.

I grin. "You look great! What are you doing in Granite Cove? Are you visiting your parents?" How long has it been since I've seen or talked to Jackie? We slowly drifted apart after high school, but she was still a bridesmaid at my wedding. Was that the last time I saw her? We talked on the phone at least, didn't we? When did that stop?

She hugs me with a laugh. "They're in Florida. I finally

convinced them to make the move permanent because it was just getting too much for them to come back here for the summers and the house stood empty for the rest of the year. I'm in town to sell it and tie up any loose ends for them. What about you? In town for a visit?"

"I live here, actually. I moved back almost two years ago."

"Wow, I didn't see that one coming. Mark left Connecticut to live in Granite Cove? It must be true love."

"Um, not so much. Mark and I divorced."

"Oh, wow, me and my big mouth. I'm sorry. Do I say sorry for the divorce too? I never know what to say when someone gets divorced because they might not be sorry at all and see it as the best thing that ever happened to them."

"That's okay, and it's definitely a good thing."

"Oh good, then congratulations! I never liked him anyway."

I laugh and rub her arm. "I've missed you. Why did we lose touch?"

She shrugs. "Life. Are you free for lunch? I'm starving."

"Yes, that would be great." I point up the block. "There's the café." I point farther up the street. "Or Flannigan's Pub."

"Let's go to the café. It's closer and my feet are killing me." She glances down at my feet. "I've never understood how you can walk around in heels all the time. I love these boots, but the skinny three-inch heels literally make me weep by the end of the day."

"They are gorgeous boots." I gaze down at my own three-inch powder blue shoes. "I think I might have permanently damaged the nerve endings in my feet. Sometimes I catch myself walking up on my tippy toes even when I'm walking barefoot around my apartment. It's as if my feet have permanently frozen in that position."

Jackie giggles as we walk into the café. "I want the added inches to my five-foot four height, but not the pain. I always felt like a shrimp standing next to you."

"I'm only five-eight."

"Yes, but you always wore at least three-inch heels. And do you remember the shoes you wore for prom? I don't comprehend how you even walked in those. I would've broken an ankle at the very least. It must be genetic. You got high-heel wearing feet and I got flat feet."

I chuckle as we stop in front of the counter at the back and stare at the chalkboard menu. "I'm not sure if that's actually a thing. Franny shares the same genetics and hates wearing heels."

Jackie grabs my arm. She stares at me with widened eyes. "How is Franny? My mom told me she married Mitch Atwater!"

"She did, and she's blissfully happy."

"Wow, she was always so quiet. If anyone was going to marry a gorgeous celebrity, I thought for sure it would've been you."

"Um, thanks, I think."

Jackie orders a sandwich and a diet soda. I order my usual salad and seltzer. We choose a small table by the front window of the narrow restaurant.

"What made you move back to Granite Cove? I would've thought you'd choose a big city to practice law in, not a small town and certainly not this one. We couldn't wait to get out of here when we were kids."

"Mark isn't the only change I made. I no longer practice law either. I'm a wedding planner now."

She blinks at me several times. "I can totally see that, actually."

"You can?"

"Sure, you always loved looking through those bride and wedding magazines. Remember how we'd go to the store and stand in front of the magazine racks after school?"

"Yes, now that you mention it, I do. I'd forgotten about that." I take a sip of my seltzer. "What about you? Last I remember, you were going to rule Wall Street with your financial genius."

Jackie slaps the table and cackles. "I did say that, didn't I?"

She shakes her head. "That seems like a lifetime ago, and I'm only thirty."

"That's right, you're an April baby. Happy birthday!"

"Thanks."

The server delivers our orders, and Jackie and I each take a bite. It is funny how long a single decade can feel when you reflect on it. I never could've predicted how my life would change or turn out back in high school.

"I still work in finance, but in Boston, not Manhattan." She shrugs. "I'm not changing the world or anything. I just manage people's portfolios."

"Do you enjoy it?"

She wrinkles her nose. "I guess so. I mean I enjoy working with numbers. I like helping people plan for their retirement."

"That's good. I hated being a lawyer. Bored the heck out of me."

She smiles and takes a bite of her sandwich. "No kids?"

"No. You? Did you get married?"

"Nope to both. I just ended a two-year relationship. He wouldn't commit. I don't mean marriage. I could've lived with not getting married, but he wouldn't even agree to move in together. After two years? If he wasn't sure I'm the one by then, he was never going to be."

"I'm sorry, that must've been difficult."

"That's the thing—it wasn't. Not really. Once I made the decision and confronted him on it, an enormous weight lifted off me."

"Then it was the right decision."

"Exactly. I think we just fell into a pattern neither of us wanted to end. We still talk. He was right not to commit."

"Look at us, two single ladies."

She raises and lowers her eyebrows. "What's the dating scene in Granite Cove? You must have all the eligible—and not so eligible—men chasing after you, like always."

"Ah, yeah, not so much. It's been a year since the divorce was final and almost two years since I told him I wanted a divorce, but I haven't been on a single date."

"Why not? Are you still pining for Mark?"

"No, not at all. He killed any love I had for him with his infidelity."

"Jackass. I hope you took him for all he's worth in the divorce."

"No, his family made sure I signed a prenup. I got my share of the house and that's about it."

"No alimony?"

"I probably could've gotten something, but I just wanted to cut all ties."

She purses her lips and takes a bite of her sandwich. Why is everyone so surprised when they find out I didn't pursue any alimony from Mark? If I had, he would've used it as an excuse to keep in touch. He still calls me every once in a while. He says it's just to check in, but I think he wants to see if I'm still single.

"Who still lives in Granite Cove? I know Kate still lives here. She married Heath and has two kids."

"Yes, I ran into her at the grocery store last year. She had her hands full with the two little ones. I guess I didn't keep in touch with anyone from high school. I don't know what anyone else is doing." I frown. I've been so wrapped up in my own life. I told Kate we should get together, but I never followed up.

"Bobby still lives in town. Mom mentions him. Have you talked to him?"

I look out the window. "You could say that."

"Oh my God! Are you dating him? Wait a minute, you said you haven't dated anyone."

"I'm not, and it definitely wouldn't be Bobby Calvert if I was. He hates my guts."

"What? Why? Oh." Jackie leans back in her chair and winces.

"What?"

She rubs the side of her neck and looks up at the ceiling. "I think I might have something to do with that."

"You? Why?"

"Umm...well...you remember I dated him our junior year, right?"

"Of course."

"I was really insecure in high school. And I was jealous of you."

"Me? Why? We were friends. I don't understand. And what does that have to do with Bobby?"

"Because I would complain about you to him. Like how you told me not to try out for cheerleading because I didn't have any coordination or the right body type for the uniform. Or how you would use my fat body as a shield to hide behind from people you didn't want to talk to."

My jaw drops. "I...no. No! Jackie, I'm so sorry. That's not true. You weren't fat. I'm so sorry if I said or did anything to make you feel that way."

Did I tell her not to try out for cheerleading? I don't remember that at all. I would never have told her that, would I? "I'm so sorry, Jackie. I don't remember any of that. If I said those things to you..." I shake my head. "Was I such a horrible person to you? A horrible friend?"

"No, you weren't. I think you could just be oblivious and thoughtless sometimes. I've had years of therapy to help me see my perspective was skewed by own insecurities and jealousies."

I drop my head into my hands. "God, no wonder Bobby hates me. I must've been one of the mean girls in high school. Why don't you hate me?" I snap my head up. "Wait, do you hate me?"

Jackie snorts out a laugh. "Lucinda, you were not one of the mean girls. You never did anything maliciously. You didn't deliberately set out to hurt someone. And I don't hate you. I may have complained to my boyfriend a little too much though.

It seems a little over the top for him to hate you for that though. I'll talk to him and explain."

"No, don't. He'll just think I put you up to it. I don't care if he doesn't like me." *At least I'm trying not to care.* "I would care if you didn't like me though. I'm really sorry, Jackie."

She stands and opens her arms for a hug. I wrap my arms around her and we sway back and forth for a minute.

"I want us to stay in touch."

"We will. I'll be in town for a couple of weeks taking care of listing my parents' house. Besides, I'm sure I'll have to come back repeatedly until it sells. We should do lunch or dinner later in the week." She pulls her phone out of her tote. "Give me your number."

I rattle off my phone number and enter hers in my phone. "Have you hired a realtor yet?"

"No, any recommendations?"

"I'll check for you. Just don't use Vanessa Michaels. She was awful to Franny growing up."

"Don't worry, I won't. She *was* one of the mean girls."

"Really? How did I not know that? Until Franny told me about all the horrible things Vanessa did to her, I had no idea. I guess I really was oblivious and self-involved."

"You didn't know because Vanessa would never have dared treat you that way. You were popular and two years older. Don't beat yourself up about something that happened in high school. We were kids."

"It's not a pretty picture."

"It never is when we look back and really analyze ourselves. None of us are perfect. Besides, it's how we act in the present that matters. I can already tell you're different. You've matured. In the past, you wouldn't have asked me about my life."

Ouch. Unfortunately, she's probably right.

CHAPTER 3

The digital scale turns on when I tap it with my toe. The zero flashes on the screen. I bite my bottom lip and gingerly step on the scale with my feet planted toward the top of the scale because, for some inexplainable reason, the scale is always kinder when I stand this way. *Please be down. Please be down.*

Nope—up two whole pounds from last week. Unbelievable! I ate a salad like a rabbit practically every day! Okay, I had a cupcake from the bakery. And a blueberry muffin, but only the top.

I glance between the scale and the bathroom window. How satisfying would it be to chuck the scale right out the window?

With my luck, it would hit someone on the head and they would sue. Or worse, it would kill them and they would arrest me for murder. Technically manslaughter, because how could you possibly prove premeditated murder by a scale? I might get off with temporary insanity if the judge and most of the jury were women.

Those two pounds make a total twenty-pound weight gain since I moved back to Granite Cove. I scrub my face with my hands. Most of my dresses are getting too tight. I've been meaning to join the gym since I moved into the apartment. It *is* right across the street. I don't have any excuse not to.

No time like the present. If I don't do it now, I never will.

I dig through my drawers for some exercise clothes. Of course, they're buried at the very bottom. Except for the couple pairs of yoga pants I own—which I've never actually done yoga in—I haven't worn exercise clothes since before I left Connecticut.

At least the pretty blue swirl pattern on the pants matches my eyes. If I'm going to exercise in public, I want to look good doing it. The pants are snug. I have to do a couple of squats and leg pulls to get them in place. Does that count as a warmup?

Twenty minutes later—all right, more like thirty—I stand on the small landing outside my door. I tighten my ponytail and wiggle my toes. The sneakers I located at the back of my closet are a little snug. I can do this. I even remembered to wear waterproof makeup in case I sweat.

I peek in the back of the bakery as I walk past. Franny pulls a tray from the oven. I wave, but she doesn't see me. I wish her schedule allowed her to join the gym with me. Although, it would hardly make sense for her to join when Mitch built a full exercise room in their house.

As I walk across the crosswalk, I glance up and down Main Street. I could just take a walk instead. It's a beautiful May day, finally warm enough to go without a coat. Isn't walking supposed to be the best exercise?

No, I'd end up ducking into the shops and getting distracted. Besides, I promised myself I would join the gym, and that's what I'm going to do.

I glance up to the top level of the plaza where the gym is located. A man in a white tank top and gray gym shorts jogs up the steps as I cross the square parking lot inside the wrap-around plaza. He's got muscled arms and a yummy backside.

With that kind of view, it might motivate me to visit the gym every day.

A smiling brunette with a long braid sits behind the desk inside the double doors. "Good morning."

"Good morning. I want to join. How do I do that?"

"Great! We've got a seven-day trial period. You can use all the facilities for free for seven days. That includes the classes. Do you want a tour?"

"Sure."

She points out the classrooms, locker rooms, and the main room with all the equipment. "You can sign up for the classes at the kiosk, our website, or download our app. As long as the class isn't full, they will allow walk-ins. Questions?"

"No, thank you. I think I'll start in here and then decide about a class later." The classes I saw in session were a little intense for my first day.

"Great! Remember to wipe down the equipment when you're done, and if you have questions, just ask one of the trainers."

A dozen or so people, about an equal mix of men and women, are using the various equipment. I guess Saturday mornings are a busy time. The same man I noticed going up the steps lifts weights in the corner. Is the front as impressive as the back? Too bad he's facing away again.

I wander over to a section with smaller handheld weights. This looks like a good place to start. I'll do a few bicep curls and scope out the rest of the machines and decide what to do. I pick up the smallest set and lift and lower. Not too bad. I can do this.

"Hey blondie, you're doing it wrong."

My head snaps up. A woman wearing a black T-shirt with "trainer" blazoned across her chest stands across the room next to a redhead in a hot pink sports bra and tight shorts. Is she talking to me? I glance around me. Yup, I'm the only blonde, and she's definitely looking in this direction.

"Form is everything. You're not checking your nails. Keep your head up, back straight, elbows back, pelvis loose, and tighten those biceps as you lift and lower."

My face heats, but I follow her instructions. Couldn't she walk over instead of bellowing across the entire room so everyone can hear?

I scan the room. Sure enough, almost everyone's gaze is on me. Even a familiar pair of brown eyes in the mirror diagonally across from me.

Bobby Calvert's reflection stares back at me with a definite smirk on his face. I drop my gaze.

He's the man I admired earlier in the white tank. Ugh, can this day get any worse?

I glance toward the exit. How pathetic would it be if I left now?

No, I will not let him or that trainer chase me away. I wipe off the weights and put them away. Fifteen minutes on a treadmill ought to be enough for everyone's attention to be elsewhere and for me to regain some dignity.

Unless of course, the display resembles a jet engine and I don't understand how to turn the damn machine on. I stare at the range of buttons while I pretend to be getting my stance just right.

After locating the start button, I press and grit my teeth. I graduated law school magna cum laude and passed the bar. I am a reasonably intelligent woman, so surely I can operate a treadmill. What's the worst that could happen? It's not like I'm going to step on it and get propelled into the window behind me, right?

I hold my breath as the belt moves and I step on. This isn't so bad. I knew I could do this.

A few minutes later, the woman in the hot pink barely-there outfit gets on the treadmill next to mine and programs the machine in a series of rapid beeps. She starts off at a jog.

Hasn't she ever heard of a warmup?

I push the speed arrow up on my machine. It beeps twice.

She pushes a button on hers and the incline of her machine increases.

I locate the incline button on my machine and hit it once, then twice.

Her machine beeps and she breaks into a full out run.

Are you kidding me?

I guess the jog was her warmup.

The back of my neck is already perspiring and my breaths are coming closer together, but I hit the incline and speed buttons one more time.

She's pumping her arms. I'm holding on to the machine with one hand praying my shoelace doesn't come untied and get stuck in the machine or that I misstep and trip off the machine and bump into her or the man next to me and cause a pileup of bodies and injuries.

My legs are warm. My shirt is sticking to my back. I'm puffing like an old steam engine. If she's the slightest bit winded, I can't hear it over my own labored breathing.

"Hi, Bobby."

Nope, she's not the slightest bit winded.

Bobby stops in front of her machine. "Hi Tanya." He wipes a towel over the back of his neck. His blond hair curls over his forehead. There's a sheen of perspiration on his tan skin.

My sneaker hits the hard side of the treadmill instead of the turning mat. I slap my other hand onto the machine and glare at my feet. *Do not trip!*

"You want to get a drink after you're done?"

How can she not be out of breath? She's running and having a conversation as if she's standing still.

The tips of his white sneakers come into view. He must be moving closer to her machine. "Can't. I've got work to catch up on. Raincheck?"

"You bet!" She sounds like she's going to break into a cheer or something.

I was a cheerleader in school, captain in fact, and I never sounded that bubbly.

"See you around." His shoes walk out of view.

Are they dating?

I lower the incline and speed on my machine. I've done twenty minutes. My chest actually aches from my labored breathing and sweat drips in my eyes. I think my ankles are even sweating.

I walk at a slower pace for a couple more minutes before stepping off the machine and shutting it down. I wipe off the machine and then stand with my hands on my hips for a minute to catch my breath.

Tanya looks over at me. Her eyes widen and a snort of laughter escapes her before she turns away.

I officially dislike this woman and I don't even know her.

What is she laughing at? The fact that I'm so out of shape a fast walk on a small incline makes me sweat and huff and puff like I've climbed a mountain? Not everyone can be superwoman like she apparently is. At least she's finally begun to sweat.

I walk over to the complimentary water station and chug two full cups of water.

Mission accomplished. I can now walk out of here with my head held high.

I smile at the woman behind the desk as I turn toward the lady's locker room to freshen up before I leave. A woman frowns at me as she passes by. Do I know her? She doesn't look familiar.

The lockers and showers are to the left. I go to the right and the row of sinks and wet a paper towel with cold water and place it on the back of my neck. I look in the mirror and let out a loud gasp. I look like a melted wax figurine.

I guess that makeup wasn't waterproof after all.

I wave my hand in front of the dispenser, grab paper towels, and scrub my face clean with the hand soap. My mother would be horrified. I can picture her just over my shoulder lecturing me on proper skin care.

She would be even more horrified to see me walk out in public without a shred of makeup on. I wipe my face dry and stare in the mirror. I haven't gone out without makeup since I was a teenager. My mother inspected my face before I left the house every day.

Why do I feel so naked?

I take a breath and scan around me. There's no one else here. Water runs in the shower area, so someone must be showering. I just walked across a gym full of people looking like something out of a horror film. I can certainly walk across the street with no makeup on.

CHAPTER 4

*M*itch and Franny's gate swings open after I punch my code in. When Franny called and invited me to lunch, I didn't hesitate to say yes. I need some sister therapy. With Mitch away until tomorrow, it'll be just the two of us.

There's a familiar truck in the driveway with Calvert Landscaping on the door. I groan. Since when does Bobby Calvert do their landscaping? Does he do everyone's in town? At least I won't have to see or talk to him. I'll park and dart inside.

Franny stands on the side of the house chatting with Bobby. I sigh and park my car. How rude would it be if I just walked inside? I could pretend not to see them over there. They're both all smiles. He throws his back in a laugh. Maybe they won't even notice. I climb out of my car with my gaze firmly fixed on the door. She wouldn't have locked it, right? What was the code? Walking into a locked door would only add to the string of embarrassing impressions I've made in front of that man.

"Luce, over here!"

I paste a smile on my face and turn toward them. Franny

waves her arm with a big smile on her face. Bobby's smile has disappeared.

"Hey, sis." I kiss her on the cheek. "Bobby."

He gives me a simple nod.

"I want to put in a small rose garden. Bobby is patiently listening to my uninformed descriptions about what I want. I don't know the names of any of them."

"You don't need to know the names. That's my job. I wouldn't know the first thing about baking one of those delicious treats you make either."

Is Bobby still carrying a torch for my sister? He did ask her out before she started dating Mitch.

"Oh, wait! I have pictures. I printed them out." She taps him on his arm. "I'll run inside and get them. Luce, keep him company."

She jogs to the house and disappears inside before I can offer to get them instead. *Great.*

"So, how are you? Have you been doing their landscaping long?"

"Can the chitchat, princess." He folds his arms over his chest. "Fake as a politician."

"Excuse me for having manners and not being a boorish, insufferable caveman!"

He snorts. "Manners? Pretending like you give a shit and asking empty questions isn't manners. It's a sham and meaningless. Shame your sister got all the personality." He pulls his phone out of his pocket. "I have to make a phone call. Go practice your fake smiles and fake manners somewhere else."

I stare at his back for a moment as tears threaten. I whirl away and stride to the door. Franny walks out as I reach for the handle.

She frowns. "Everything okay?" She glances over at Bobby and back at me.

"Just peachy. I'm going to wait inside, okay?"

"Of course. I'll only be a few more minutes."

I nod and walk inside. I walk down the long hallway to the kitchen and pour myself a glass of water. Am I fake? Is it really so wrong to be polite?

Just because I smile when I'd rather not doesn't make me fake. Should I have told him to go to hell instead?

And they weren't empty questions. I *was* wondering how long he's worked for them.

The front door opens and closes. Please let Franny be alone and not with Bobby.

Bobby, not Bob. Why does a thirty-year-old man still go around calling himself Bobby?

"Hey, what's going on?"

Franny stands in the open doorway, frowning.

"Am I fake? Is that how people see me?"

"What? No, of course not! Did Bobby say that to you?"

"Among other things."

"What is it with you two? Is there a history I don't know about? He's always so friendly, except when you're around. I don't get it."

"Neither did I, so I asked him point blank. He said he just doesn't like me. I ran into Jackie last week, and she told me when they were dating, she told him about some of the not-so-pleasant things I said to her when we were in high school. I feel awful. I never realized I was such a bitch. Was I horrible to you, too?"

Franny hugs me. "Don't be silly. You're not a bitch, and you've always been a wonderful sister to me. If you were a bitch, you wouldn't feel awful about making her feel bad back then. And you're not fake. You're kind and charming. You're an extrovert. You're good with people. If Bobby doesn't like you because of something you inadvertently said to Jackie back in high school, then he's a jerk. Makes me think I shouldn't have lobbied so hard to Mitch for us to hire him."

"Don't change your opinion of him because of me. He said I can't stand that someone doesn't like me, and he's right. I don't understand why it bothers me so much. Why do I care so much what other people think of me?"

"You really have to ask? It's all thanks to our mother."

"She raised us both and you're not like that. I was afraid to leave the gym without makeup on. I thought I might have a panic attack over it."

"She was always different with me than with you. With you, she expected perfection. With me, she just hoped I wouldn't embarrass her with my presence." Franny squeezes my hands. "Luce, you're an incredibly beautiful woman, with or without makeup. It's okay if you wear makeup everywhere and it's okay if you don't, as long as it's your decision. Don't do it because you feel you need to put on a mask. Do it because it makes you feel good."

I lay my head on her shoulder. "When did you get so wise?"

"It's always easier to give someone else advice than to give it to yourself. Our visions of ourselves are often skewed. I used to be terrified of people and their reactions so much that I avoided them instead." She shrugs. "I still do sometimes. But now it's not so much because I'm afraid of other people; it's because I'm an introvert. You need to decide what makes you happy and follow your own path." She opens the fridge. "Now, I don't know about you, but I'm starving. How about some lunch?"

"Good idea. Let's talk about something else. Like when the construction on my new deck is going to start." Her expansion of the bakery's outdoor seating includes a bigger deck on the upstairs apartment.

Franny laughs. "Actually, that's one reason I invited you to lunch. I have the plans and the contractor wants to start next week. Let me grab the sandwiches I made and I'll show you while we eat."

She hands me the sandwiches and I carry them over to the

eating nook while she walks out of the room. She returns with a tablet.

"He sent me the plans in full color. It looks like a painting or something." She sits on the bench across from me, taps on the tablet, and slides it across the table to me.

The back patio connects to the front patio with a wide brick pathway that matches the existing front patio. It's wide enough for a single row of black wrought-iron tables and chairs and the pathway. There's potted flowers and bushes lining the walkway.

"He needed to stay a certain distance from the property line so it's kind of narrow on the side, but the back will be where most of the added seating will be." Franny takes a bite of her sandwich.

"Makes sense. The back has the view, anyway."

The back patio will span the entire building with potted shrubs lining the sides. It'll provide a windbreak and block most of the parking lot on one side and the buildings next door on the other. They will move my stairs to the other side of the building with a deck all the way across. I'll have room for not only the table and chairs I wanted, but I could fit a whole other seating area.

"He's going to do your deck in stages, so you always have access to your apartment. And your deck will provide some shade for the tables underneath. I told him to add a gate to the bottom of your stairs too, so nobody thinks your deck is another public space."

"Franny, this is amazing. It looks beautiful, and I absolutely love the new deck you're adding." I put a hand to my chest and wink. "Of course, I might be a little bias about that since I'm already planning how I'll decorate it."

She laughs. "Good. I'm excited too. I've wanted to expand the seating at the bakery for a while. Olivia started interviewing last week. She estimates we'll need at least two more part-timers for the summer."

"Expand away! I'm getting an entire new living space out of it. Are you going to raise my rent?"

"Of course not!"

"You should. I already told you a lakeview apartment rents higher than what you charge me. With this new deck, you should probably charge me double." I try not to cringe as I say it. I really can't afford double the rent. At least not until my business gets a steadier clientele.

Franny shakes her head. "You're family. I'm not raising your rent. I'm perfectly happy with our arrangement. If you ever decide to move out, then I'll raise the rent before I find another tenant."

"I'm pretty sure you're stuck with me for the foreseeable future."

"Good. I enjoy having you right upstairs over the bakery so you can drop in and see me whenever you want."

"Me too." I pull my knee up on the bench and take a bite of my sandwich. "Mmm. This is so good. What is it?" I peer at the ham and cheese sandwich.

"It's a new aioli. Good, right?"

"So good." I take another bite.

"I made one of your favorites for dessert—tiramisu."

I groan. I guess I'm going to have to drag my ass back to the gym after all. I had almost convinced myself I could buy some equipment and work out at home instead. But I know I won't. I need the monetary commitment of a gym membership and the shame hanging over my head if I don't show up.

CHAPTER 5

I sink into a warrior pose and glance down at the yoga mat to make sure I point my toes in the correct direction. Warm hands slide down my sides.

"A little lower, Lucinda. Feel the burn in your thighs?" Brody moves his hands to my biceps. "Lengthen your arms."

I stretch my arms further and give him a sideways glance. My thighs are indeed burning.

His hazel eyes sparkle above his wide smile. Brody's handsome face and extremely toned body helped convince me to sign up for this yoga class. A pleasant view helps the class go by quicker. And it turns out I actually enjoy yoga. It's a great stress reliever. I haven't seen the pounds melting away, but it's only been a few classes.

"Great job. Your body's getting stronger." Brody gives me a wink and weaves his way through the mats and people to the front of the room.

I peek at my arms as I move into downward dog. There might be a little more muscle definition.

My cheek rests against the mat when we finish the session with child's pose. Brody has been giving me more and more hands-on direction over the last couple of classes. Is he flirting with me? It's not like I'm the only person he gives attention to in class. There are a few women who constantly ask him for direction. One, in particular, I know doesn't need any help with the poses. She could probably run the class herself the way she moves through all the different poses without a single stumble or wobble. It's clear she just wants his personal attention. She's always flirting with him before and after class, too. I've never seen him encourage her advances, though.

Could he be my first foray back into dating? I certainly like when he puts his hands on me. Of course, it's been so long since any man has that my body might be a little starved for attention.

Everyone stands and grabs their mats. There are the typical few women surrounding Brody at the front of the room. I roll up my mat and stroll toward the door. I don't want to hang around him like some groupie.

"Hey, Lucinda, hold up a minute." Brody waves me over. "Goodbye, ladies. Have a great day!"

The small crowd disperses with a few pouts and glares in my direction.

Is he going to ask me out? Should I say yes?

"You've got a knack for this. You should take my more advanced class. It's a full hour."

"Oh, you really think so?"

He tilts his head and starts walking toward the door. "You're naturally flexible. You've picked up the moves quickly. I think you might get more out of the longer class."

"Thanks. I enjoy your classes." I pause at the door opening. "Brody, would you like to get coffee some time?"

"I make it a rule not to get involved with clients. But you should definitely come to my other class." He smiles and walks away.

There's a snort behind me. My cheeks burn as I whirl around. Bobby smirks at me from a few feet away.

Great! Not only was I turned down, but the one person I'd rather avoid is there to witness my embarrassment.

"Eavesdropping? Isn't that rather beneath you?"

"Gotta admit, that was entertaining as hell—better than TV."

"I'm so glad my humiliation is entertaining to you."

"What's the matter, princess? Hasn't a guy ever told you no before?" He chuckles and folds his arms over his chest.

"If you must know, he's the first guy I've ever asked out." And I'll keep my mouth shut from now on. I'd rather become a spinster than experience this awful, weighted mass churning around in my stomach again.

"It's called rejection. Now you understand how all the guys you've turned down have felt."

My scowl turns into a frown. I've always tried to be gentle any time I've said no to a guy. Kind of like how Brody just let me down easy. It could've gone much worse.

"I know what rejection feels like, Bobby. My husband cheated on me—repeatedly. There, you can enjoy that knowledge too." I march past him.

My yoga mat slips out from underneath my swinging arm and rolls across the hallway. I scramble to snatch it up so I can get the hell out of here before Bobby can deliver any more cutting remarks.

His tan arm grabs the edge of my blue mat before I can and rolls it up. "Don't feel too bad, princess, he's gay. Asked me out last year." He hands me my mat.

I take my mat from him and frown. "Thanks." I turn to go but swing back. "You could've just let me go on feeling bad. Why didn't you?"

He shrugs. "Unlike some people, I don't get enjoyment out of intentionally hurting people."

"I suppose that's a dig on me. After speaking to Jackie recently, I realize I wasn't always a very good friend to her in high school. That's between her and me. I've made my apologies. I'm not proud of some things I did in high school."

"You mean like how you dumped Sal right before prom so you could go with a college guy instead?"

My mouth drops open and I rear back from him. "I don't know what he told you, but that's not what happened." I shove past him and make a beeline for the exit.

Tears fill my eyes. Salvatore Rosetti. That lying little troll! He's the one who told me to find someone else to take me to prom. Basically gave me an ultimatum of having sex with him or finding someone else for my date. He didn't think I could find someone else a week before prom. Like I would ever let some idiot jock who thought he was God's gift to women manipulate me into having sex before I was ready.

I swipe at the tear pooled in the corner of my eye as I stalk across the crosswalk. What other lies did he spread about me?

We'd started dating earlier that year, and I knew it wasn't going anywhere. It was high school. We were both going off to college soon. And his ego had already gotten old, but prom was looming, so I didn't break up with him. Then he got drunk at a party and was pissed when I said no once again. He'd given me the ultimatum and stormed off. He probably thought I'd go crawling back to him rather than find someone else. Jerk! Did he really think I couldn't find someone else so quickly? There were a few guys I could have asked from school. But I wanted to show him what he could do with his stupid ultimatum. The next day I went over to the college campus bookstore and had a date in less than an hour. Maybe I was petty, but he deserved it.

I stomp up the stairs to my apartment. And Bobby is a jerk too! Condemning me for things he thought I did in high school —who the hell does he think he is? Was he so perfect? Didn't he ever make mistakes?

He says he doesn't get enjoyment out of hurting others, but obviously he does. At least he enjoys hurting me.

I toss my yoga mat into the corner and it opens with a splat. I slump into the chair in my living room and drum my fingers on the arm of the chair.

Was I supposed to slink off and miss my senior prom because some guy thought I owed it to him to have sex with him? Men are such idiots.

I close my eyes and drop my head back. It was high school and over a decade ago. Who cares what happened back then? If Bobby wants to hate me for what he thinks happened back then, then so be it.

A hard knock raps at my door.

Franny or Olivia probably heard or saw me tromp up the stairs and came to check on me. Or one of them just wants to chat. I could use some girl time and someone else's perspective.

I swing open the door. It's not Franny or Olivia. Bobby frowns at me from my porch.

My fingers tighten on the doorknob. I could just swing it closed in his face. He deserves it. He's always so nasty to me and nice to everyone else. I sigh and lift my chin. Nope, not going to sink to his level. I'm taking the high road.

"Listen, I'm not the same person I was in high school and I shouldn't be judging you based on how you were in high school. I was out of line, and I'm sorry."

My shoulders deflate. That was unexpected. "Thank you." I guess. I mean, he's still basically saying I was a horrible person in high school even though I didn't do some things he thinks I did.

Bobby nods. "Look, we live in the same town, and we're bound to run into each other once in a while. I can be civil if you can dial back the fake, bouncing, bubbly Barbie routine."

I plant my hand on my hip as the urge to slam the door in his face resurfaces. Fake, bouncy, bubbly Barbie? Is that how he sees me?

"You call a truce by insulting me? I'm not fake, bouncy,

bubbly, or a Barbie! Yes, I try to be pleasant and friendly. There's nothing wrong with that. Having manners is not fake. If you weren't such a nasty, brooding son-of-a-bitch, you might realize that!"

I slam the door in his face.

It bounces open and hits me on the shoulder.

Pain ricochets down my arm. I grab my shoulder and wince. Are you kidding me? I can't even slam a door properly without it backfiring.

"You're probably going to want to put ice on that. Got any?" He walks past me into my apartment and into the tiny kitchen tucked into the corner behind the door. He grabs an ice tray out of the freezer and a paper towel from under the cabinet.

He's getting me ice?

Bobby slaps the ice wrapped in a paper towel into my hand.

"Thanks." I gingerly place it on my shoulder and wince over the cold.

He props his fists on his hips and gazes around my apartment. If one nasty comment comes out of his mouth, I'm throwing this ice in his face.

"I guess I owe you another apology."

"You guess?"

"All right, I do. I'm sorry. I shouldn't have called you that."

I sigh. "I'm sorry too. I shouldn't have called you names either."

The corner of his mouth twitches up briefly. "How's the shoulder?"

"If you laugh, I might have to hit you." I glare at him.

"Think they'd call that assault."

"Self-defense."

"Aren't you a lawyer? Doesn't sound like you have a case."

"Not anymore. I think you'd have a tough time getting a police officer to arrest me. Besides, with my luck, I'd probably break my hand or something if I hit you."

"Never saw you as the violent type. Doesn't jibe with the whole Barbie vibe."

"I am not a Barbie!" I stalk into the kitchen and toss the ice into the sink. "Not even my ex-husband made me this mad!"

"I didn't mean it as an insult—exactly. It's the positive, smiling blondness that wants everyone to like them look." He holds up his hands. "I'll try to refrain from calling you that, okay?"

I roll my eyes and lean against the sink.

"You said he cheated on you. You didn't get mad?"

"Seriously?"

"What? I find it hard to believe I make you madder than your cheating ex-husband."

"I was mad the first time and the second. But after a while, I slipped into a state of numbness and denial. If I ignored it, I could pretend my marriage wasn't over and I wasn't a failure."

"If he's the one who cheated, why would you be a failure?"

"Have you ever been married?"

He shakes his head.

"It's hard to explain. I realize he's the one who cheated, but it made me question myself and wonder if I had done something or not done something to make him look elsewhere. I never thought I would be divorced, let alone after only a few years of marriage."

"I think you're looking at it wrong. You didn't waste your life tied to an asshole. You got out and started over. Now you have your whole life in front of you."

I tilt my head to the side. "So you can be nice to me after all." I peek out the window behind me. "The sun is still shining. The world didn't end. Look at that."

"Funny. I better get out of here before I say something to break the truce."

I close the door behind him—softly this time.

CHAPTER 6

"Oh, you realize how it is. Lucinda needed some time off after the divorce. She's deciding between practicing law here in New Hampshire or going back to Connecticut. She even has offers in New York." Mother cradles the phone against her ear while she checks her reflection in the mirror over the living room couch.

I fold my arms over my waist and lean against the entryway. So, now she's outright lying to people about me. I shouldn't be surprised and I'm not, not really. She's never been shy about showing her disappointment and displeasure over any of my decisions that don't agree with her vision of my life.

She chuckles. "Yes, wouldn't that be lovely? I'd have an excuse to make more regular trips to Manhattan and do some shopping." She turns and spots me in the doorway. The smile falls from her face. "I'll talk to you later, Betsy. Someone is at the door."

"Spreading lies, Mother? You do recall Betsy lives in town and is bound to hear I'm a wedding planner now, not a lawyer, and that I have no intention of going back to practicing. How are you going to explain that? More lies?"

Mother's pointed chin lifts higher like she's aiming a weapon at me and a laser will shoot out any second. What a terrifying thought, my mother with a laser weapon she could fire at will. She would've vaporized us years ago.

"You've had your little rebellion. It's time to get back to reality and give up this silly notion of becoming a wedding planner. Your father and I didn't make sacrifices and send you to college so you could throw away your whole life planning other people's weddings." Mother throws her hands up in the air and paces across the living room.

"If being a lawyer is so important to you, why don't *you* go to law school? I enjoy helping brides and grooms plan their special day. It makes me happy. Don't you want me to be happy?"

"Grow up, Lucinda! No one is happy! That's life! At least as a lawyer, you'll have your dignity and a stable income. If you think your father and I are going to support your ridiculous endeavor, you're sadly mistaken."

"I think that's a very depressing outlook on life, Mother. And I haven't asked you for a dime. My business is actually profitable, much sooner than I had hoped. I'm looking to rent a business space."

Her lips tighten and narrow. "I don't understand where I went so wrong with you and your sister. You both had every advantage. Yet you choose to squander everything we've given you. You're both ungrateful."

"Franny runs a successful business and is ridiculously happy. How could you possibly say she's squandered anything? Just because she chose a different path than the one you wanted for her? I think you're the ungrateful one, Mother. You have two daughters pursuing their dreams. You should be happy for them. You should be down on your knees thanking God Franny still puts up with you and allows you into her life at all after the way you've treated her. Is that your goal, Mother? Drive your daughters away permanently with your constant disapproval and criticism of the lives we've chosen for ourselves? If you end up all alone, you'll have no one to blame but yourself." I scan the room full of expensive antiques and collectibles. It's as cold and unwelcoming as she is. "Goodbye, Mother. Your shameful daughter has an appointment with a happy bride."

Glass shatters in the living room as I stalk out the front door. Tears burn at the back of my eyes and my chest feels like I made another attempt to run on a treadmill.

Bobby stands in front of the bushes lining the living room windows. He's wearing gloves and has a set of giant clippers in his hands. The metal snaps as he clips the tip of a branch. He spares me a glance and then squints up at the sun.

Would it be too much to hope he didn't hear any of that?

"My first month on the job, your mother would walk around the yard critiquing my work. She had me take notes and would review those notes. She must've fired me a dozen times that first year, but your father always hired me back."

Yup, he heard. "Sounds about right. How long have you been working for my parents?"

"Since right after high school."

That long? And I never noticed. Jackie was right. I guess I am oblivious. I shake my head and stare up at the blue sky with giant, puffy white clouds. I could make the excuse that I had gone off to college, but I came home for visits. Too self-involved with my own life to even notice someone I knew worked in my parents' yard.

"Dry your eyes, princess." Bobby holds out a folded white handkerchief.

I stare at the cloth dangling from his fingers and wipe at my wet cheek. When did I start crying?

"Don't worry, it's clean."

I snap my gaze up to his face and take the offering. "That's not it. I'm just surprised you carry one. My grandfather was the only man I ever saw with one."

"Yeah, my grandfather made me carry them and lectured me every time he found me without one." He shrugs. "It became a habit."

"Thank you. It's nice." I glance back at the house. "How much of that did you hear?"

"Pulled up when you walked in the door."

"So you heard everything?"

"Only when she shouted, and you shouted back."

I wince and sigh. "She's never going to change. When will I stop caring what my mother thinks?"

"Don't ask me. Mine took off when I was a kid. I stopped caring a long time ago."

Ouch! How did I not know that? "I'm sorry. I didn't know."

"Why would you?"

"Because we grew up together. The town's not that big."

"It's not exactly something I ever advertised."

I step down off the steps and onto the grass. How different would my life have been if my mother had taken off when I was a kid? No one to criticize my every move. No one to fear disappointing.

And what kind of awful person am I to think it might've been better?

My father would've been devastated, of course, but he would've remarried. He's not the type to be alone or raise two kids alone. If he has a type, I probably would've ended up with a stepmother just like her, or worse, because we wouldn't have been her daughters.

"Mind if I ask you something?"

He shrugs. "You can ask. If I don't want to answer, I won't."

"Are you happy?"

He tucks the clippers against his side and folds his arms. "Are you asking because you're wondering how a landscaper can be happy?"

I open my mouth and then snap it closed and shake my head.

"No, of course not. I'm not my mother. I just mean, do you enjoy your life? Does landscaping make you happy? Or is there something else you wish you were doing?"

"I wish I was sitting in my boat reeling in a large mouth bass." He smiles and looks over at his truck parked in front of my parents' house. "I basically fell into landscaping because I was a teenager without any skills. I needed the money. I stuck with it because I discovered I had a knack for it, and yeah, I enjoy it."

Nodding, I glance around the green yard. Manicured bushes line the front and sides of the house. There are no flowers. Mother hates the sight of dead blooms. She swaps out bouquets inside the house every few days. "I don't know the first thing about landscaping, but even I can see you're good at your job. I've seen what you've done at Franny and Mitch's house. That takes talent." Their gardens are like a park.

"Mitch took some convincing. He didn't want to hire me."

"Can you blame him? You had a thing for my sister."

"I wouldn't say it was a thing. We only went on one date, which you and Mitch interrupted."

I smile. "God, that dinner was so awkward. But it all worked out in the end. Franny and Mitch are perfect together."

"Nobody's perfect."

"What do you mean?" He couldn't possibly know something about them I don't, could he? I'd perceive if they weren't happy.

"Just that chasing perfection will only lead to disappointment."

"Oh, believe me, I'm well aware of that. That's not what I meant. I meant Mitch and Franny love each other and they'll do whatever is necessary to ensure each other's happiness. They won't sacrifice the other's happiness for their own. They put each other first before everything else."

"Yeah, they seem pretty happy together. But then, newlyweds usually are."

"That's rather cynical. Are you not a fan of marriage?"

"Never thought of it one way or the other. I just think a good marriage takes a lot of hard work and most people aren't willing to do the work, day in and day out, year after year."

"I think Franny and Mitch will be one of the couples who make it."

"Only time will tell."

"Yes, it will. Thanks for this." I wave my hand between us. "Talking. I guess the truce is working."

"About that." He squints up at the sun and turns his baseball cap back around so the brim is shading his face. "Had dinner with Jackie the other night. She told me you weren't as bad as she made you out to be. It got me thinking about Sal and how you said that wasn't what happened, either. He was a dick in high school. Probably still is. I guess what I'm trying to say is, I'm sorry. I shouldn't have based my opinion of you on hearsay."

"Bet that hurt."

He smirks. "Little bit."

"There's a reason you can't use hearsay as evidence in court."

"You're going to rub this in, aren't you?"

I smile and shake my head. "No. The truth is, I could've been better in high school. I never meant to hurt Jackie, and I should've been a better friend to her."

"We agreed to put high school in the past where it belongs. I doubt either of us is the same person we were back then." He holds out his hand. "Hi, I'm Bobby."

I slip my hand into his with a laugh. "It's nice to meet you. I'm Lucinda." I grin and tuck my hands behind my back. "So, you had dinner with Jackie the other night? Are you two becoming a couple again?"

Funny how Jackie hadn't mentioned that when I talked to her on the phone yesterday. Although, she had been on her way to the airport and was busy.

"It was just dinner. And isn't that quite a jump from introducing ourselves to asking about my dating life?"

"Not really. Jackie's my friend and now you are too. I look out for my friends."

"So now we're friends?"

"Yup." I wink. "I knew my perky personality would win you over, eventually."

I'm lying through my teeth, but he doesn't need to know that. I was pretty sure he'd dislike me forever.

He snorts out a laugh. "I called you bubbly and bouncy, not perky, but I guess they mean pretty much the same thing. And perky goes with princess better. Yeah, I like perky princess better.

I frown. "Not sure I care for that nickname. But if you don't mind me calling you Brooding Bro, or BB for short..."

"So I should call you PP?" He throws his head back and laughs.

I grimace and stare at his tanned throat. "Please don't." How did that go so wrong?

CHAPTER 7

"Okay, Monica is in charge of the venue. Which makes sense, since the baby shower is at her house." The book club ladies chuckle. "Franny and Kerry have food duty. Our stomachs thank you both. Rebecca is in charge of the invitations and keeping track of RSVPs. Sally, Aggie, and Barbara are handling games and gifts. And Kelly and I are doing the decorations. Did I miss anything? Anyone have any questions or need help completing any of their tasks? We've only got three weeks left until Tina's shower."

I glance around my small apartment. It's amazing the ten of us fit in my living room. When Tina arrives, it'll be eleven. Hopefully, we're not violating some fire code or something. Once the deck expansion is complete, we'll have more space to spread out.

Barbara tilts her head toward Sally and Aggie. "Other than keeping these two in check with the x-rated games they want to play, I think we have it under control. We're having a wrapping party at Aggie's for the gifts and prizes next week if any of you want to drop by."

Aggie cackles. "I found penis and vagina guessing games, but Barbara ruled them out."

"If it didn't have such graphic pictures, it might have been okay, but I think it's better to err on the side of caution so we don't offend any of the attendees." Barbara glances around the room. "Am I being too conservative?"

"Considering Hope is attending the shower, I think nixing the game was a good idea. I don't want to be responsible for corrupting young minds." Rebecca winks. "We'll save games like that for the next baby shower when it's just us ladies." She looks around at all of us. "Any of you ladies have news you want to share so we can start planning?"

There are a lot of negative murmurs and head shaking. I glance at Olivia. She mentioned having baby fever a while back and now that her wedding has passed, she and Luke might've decided to expand the family. She's shaking her head no as she sips her wine, though. Kelly sits next to her with pink-tinged cheeks.

I suck in a breath and glance at her belly. She has been wearing loose-fitting clothes lately. It's only been two months since their wedding in Texas. She wouldn't be showing yet. Unless she was pregnant before the wedding?

"Luce?"

"Hmm…? I glance at Franny.

"Monica asked you if you needed any help with the decorations or if there were any she needed to make space for at her house."

"Oh, sorry. I think Kelly and I have it all under control. We plan to bring that pretty throne-like antique chair Kelly has in her shop for Tina to sit in, but I don't think any of the other decorations require moving furniture around or anything. What do you think, Kelly?"

I'd been in and out of her shop pretty much once a week lately with brides or to plan the shower. She never said a thing.

I'd been there first thing in the morning before she opened once too and she didn't seem to experience morning sickness. Maybe I'm just imagining things.

Kelly shakes her head. "We've already bought everything and they're in the backroom of my shop. I think we have everything covered."

"What's going on?" Rebecca narrows her eyes and glances between Kelly and me. "Lucinda, you're staring at Kelly, and she's squirming in her seat."

Uh oh. I hope I haven't ratted Kelly out before she's ready to share. I shrug and smile. "Nothing. I was just thinking."

Kelly presses her lips together and blushes a deep red. "Well, actually, I do have some news, but I didn't want to steal any of the attention from Tina. I was going to wait until after her shower."

"I knew it!" I jump up and then cringe when everyone looks at me. "Sorry! Congratulations, Kelly!"

Everyone hugs and congratulates Kelly. Tina walks in while we're all huddled together. "What's going on? Am I late?" She glances at her watch and winces. "Sorry, I'd blame it on pregnancy brain, but you all know me too well to let that fly."

I laugh and walk over and give her a hug. "How are you feeling? You look great."

"You're too kind, Lucinda. I'm exhausted and excited at the same time."

"Sit, and I'll get you something to drink." I direct her over to one of the armchairs.

"What did I miss?" Tina glances around while I get her a drink and fill a small plate of treats from Franny's bakery.

Everyone looks at Kelly and she bites her lip. "I'm pregnant."

"Oh my God!" Tina hauls herself up from the chair and wraps her arms around Kelly. "We're pregnant together!"

"You're not mad?"

Tina frowns and tilts her head. "Why would I be mad?"

"I don't want to steal your thunder or anything."

"Don't be silly. I'm overjoyed I have someone to commiserate with when I don't understand what the heck is going on with my body." Tina puts her hands on her belly and grins. "I realize I have over a month to go, but I feel like I'm ready to pop. When are you due?"

"September."

"Ooh, your baby will be a Virgo like me." I wait for Tina to sit back down and hand her the drink and plate. "Do you know if it's a girl or a boy? Or do you and Holden want to be surprised, like Tina and Ron?" Kelly must be six months along, and she's not even really showing.

Kelly grins. "We just found out yesterday, actually. We're having a girl."

"Holden must be over the moon. Trevor too." Olivia's smile turns into a frown. "Wait, does he know? He hasn't said anything when he's been over to hang with the twins."

"He knows. He's just great at keeping secrets. He's thrilled."

Olivia chuckles. "I don't think my boys could ever keep a secret like that."

"Boy, our calendars have been overflowing with celebrations lately. We've got weddings and babies. It's wonderful!" Franny throws her hands out and laughs.

"If anyone could send some man vibes my way, I'd appreciate it. I don't need a wedding or another baby, but I wouldn't turn down a date or two." Barbara snorts out a laugh and takes a sip of her wine.

"Me too." I lift my glass of wine and then lower it. "Or maybe not. I'm not sure if I'm ready to date after all. I thought I was. I even asked a guy out for the first time in my life. Turned me down."

Rebecca mutters. "Idiot."

Franny sucks in a breath. "Oh no, who?"

"It wasn't Ollie, was it?" Olivia grimaces comically.

I wave my hand. "It sucked, but it's fine. He happens to be gay, so I felt slightly better about it. Not well enough to go back to my yoga class, though." I glance around at everyone. "He's my yoga instructor."

"Well, you can't feel bad about that. You lack the necessary anatomy." Monica shrugs and bites into a cookie.

"You should be proud of yourself for having the nerve to ask a guy out. I'm too chicken, which is why I haven't had a date in so long. I'm afraid I've forgotten how to behave around men— how to flirt." Barbara hides her face in her hands.

"Have you tried one of those dating apps?" Aggie's gaze bounces between Barbara and me.

I wrinkle my nose. "I realize that's the way people do these things nowadays, but it feels too weird to me. Like I'm shopping for a man or advertising myself to men. Am I crazy?" I glance around the room. "Is it just me? Are any of you on those apps?"

Kerry raises her hand. "I use them." She shrugs. "I can't really recommend them since I'm still single. It can feel a bit sleezy at times."

"I gave up on dating apps. But then again I go through these periods where I'll delete my profiles and then a few months go by and I'll start new ones." Monica rolls her eyes. "Makes me understand the appeal of arranged marriages. I'd like to be married, but I don't want to endure all the dating to find the right guy."

Sally leans forward and purses her lips. "You need one of those matchmakers. I saw them on TV. Don't know if there are any in Granite Cove, though."

Monica laughs. "If anyone hears about a matchmaker setting up shop in Granite Cove, let me know."

Aggie wiggles her eyebrows. "You might have something there." She bumps her arm against Sally's. "We could do something like that, don't you think? We'll start with the single gals right here in book club."

My mouth opens and closes. "Cross me off the list. I've realized I need to work on myself some more before I consider dating."

Olivia frowns. "What do you need to work on?"

"My insecurities, for one. I would never have described myself as insecure before, but do you know until recently I never set foot out the door without makeup on?" I've been slowly weaning myself off it and only wearing it for client meetings and social gatherings.

Franny shakes her head. "I told you, that's our mother's fault. I can't recall the last time I ever saw her without makeup on, and I lived with her before Mitch."

"You know, you're right. I can't remember ever seeing her without makeup, either. Not even when we were kids."

"I never used to leave the house without makeup until I had Joey. Kids change your perspective." Barbara smiles and leans forward to peek at Aggie. "I wouldn't be completely opposed to any matchmaking attempts you want to send my way."

Aggie grins and points a finger at Barbara. "You'll be our first project." She slaps Sally on the arm. "This is going to be fun."

"I certainly go around without makeup all the time." Kerry points to her bare face. "But I also think it's different for me. I mean, Lucinda, you're a beautiful woman and I'm sure you've been told that all your life. For me, people always told me how smart I am. So I get more self-conscious about my intelligence than my looks. I don't want to appear stupid because being smart has become one of my identifiers, like being beautiful is probably one of yours. Does that make any sense?"

I lean back in my chair and try not to frown too hard. "Kerry, you're a beautiful woman. Don't sell yourself short." She's let her brown hair grow out and it's below her shoulders. I'd add some blonde highlights to it, but it's thick with a slight wave. Her large, hazel eyes are always kind. "I see what you're saying, but I don't like it. I mean, beauty fades and it's subjective anyway. I don't want that to be one of my identifiers. I don't want to be that shallow. Am I that shallow?" I look at Franny.

Franny puts her hand on mine. "You're not shallow, Luce. Yes, you're beautiful, but you're smart too. You were always the smart *and* beautiful one. Look at all you've accomplished. Not only did you become a lawyer, but you've started your own business and it's already successful."

"Besides, if wearing makeup makes you feel good, then there's not a thing wrong with it. Heck, you can get makeup permanently tattooed on these days. I say go for it." Rebecca crosses her arms over her crossed knee and points her wine glass toward me. "You do you."

"That's the thing though, I don't know if it is really me and what I want or if it's just an ingrained habit because I'm afraid to be without it. I've gone to the gym without makeup a few times now and no one stared in horror." I smile and roll my eyes. "It certainly saves a lot of time getting ready. It seems like such a silly thing to obsess over, but it's a symptom, I think. It's just one detail that makes me wonder if I can be ready for a relationship."

"Not to sound dire, but perfection doesn't exist. If you wait to become the perfect you and fix all the things you perceive are wrong, then it'll be a never-ending battle. There are always new insecurities or issues popping up. If you're not ready to date, then don't date, but don't put it off because you think you need to better yourself first. It's not like you have some glaring character flaw or anything. Just my two cents." Monica pats her knees. "Now, how about we discuss the book? This is book club, after all."

CHAPTER 8

*I*s there anyone anywhere who enjoys going to the doctor? Maybe a hypochondriac or something? But really, who enjoys being poked, asked exceedingly intimate questions, basically being critiqued on your lifestyle choices? And let's not forget getting on the scale in front of someone. I sigh and stare up at the Federal style building.

The sunny yellow paint is rather charming. At least the doctor's office isn't in a sterile cement building like my previous one in Connecticut. It's just a checkup. It could be worse; it could be a gynecological visit. I don't have to spread my legs while a complete stranger sticks a cold metal instrument inside me. I climb out of my car and shut the door. I've already canceled one appointment. They'll probably drop me as a patient if I do it again, especially since this is my first visit.

Franny half-jokingly offered to come with me. Perhaps I should have said yes. Who cares if I'm going to turn thirty in a few months? Franny knows I've been afraid of doctors since I was a kid. She understands.

I stop on the sidewalk and stare at the wooden sign next to

the door. There's several doctors' names listed. They must share the building.

"Is the door locked or are you gathering strength to walk inside?" An older man in a wheelchair wheels up the ramp.

"Oh, I'm sorry." I step out of the way and open the door for him.

"Guess it was the second one, huh?" He passes by me.

"Yes, I'm not a fan of going to the doctor."

"Understandable. I only go so as not to hurt my doctor's feelings. If I don't show up, he's likely to think I don't like him or something. Now, a pretty lady like you...if you don't show up, you're likely to ruin his entire day."

I laugh. "Is that so? I don't think we have the same doctor. My doctor is a woman."

He shakes his head dejectedly. "Dr. Fox is going to be so disappointed when I tell him about the pretty lady his coworker nabbed from him."

"You're very sweet, but I think your doctor will be fine. He'll have your company to cheer him up."

The man winks. "Are you single?"

I widen my eyes and chuckle. Is he flirting with me? That would be my luck. The first man to show an interest in me in I don't remember how long and he's old enough to be my father. "As a matter of fact, I am. Are you?"

He throws his head back and lets out a belly laugh.

"Pops? You took off without me and left your wallet in the van."

I whirl around. Bobby stands behind me holding out a brown leather wallet to the man in the wheelchair. This is his father?

"I was chasing after this pretty lady. I didn't want her to disappear inside before I could say hello." He takes the wallet and dumps it in his lap.

Bobby glances at me and nods once. "Lucinda."

"Bobby." Is the truce over? He doesn't appear happy to see me.

"You two know each other?" He frowns at Bobby. "Introduce me to your lady friend." He shakes his head and smiles at me. "Bobby never brings his dates home to meet me."

Bobby sighs heavily. "She's not my…" He pinches the bridge of his nose. "Pops, this is Lucinda. We went to high school together. Lucinda, this is my father, George. I'm going to go check you in." He walks over to the window, and the pretty brunette smiles at his approach.

George holds out his hand. "In case you're not aware, my son is single, too."

I press my lips together and glance at Bobby's back as I shake George's hand. I don't think Bobby has any trouble getting dates if the woman from the gym and the flirting receptionist are anything to go by. If he's single, it's probably by choice.

"And here I thought you were asking if I was single for yourself."

He guffaws again and squeezes my hand. "I like you."

"I like you too." I glance up as Bobby walks over and then back down to his father. "I better check in, too. Thanks for distracting me enough to get me inside."

"Noticed that, did you?" He winks. "Quick and pretty. A dangerous combination. That's okay though. I like to live dangerously."

I laugh and shake my head as I walk over to the window. The receptionist's smile has significantly dimmed, but she's still polite as she checks me in for my appointment.

Bobby sits in a chair next to his father, filling out the paperwork the receptionist handed him. I did all the paperwork online, so that's at least one less thing to worry about.

George pats the arm of the chair on the other side of him. "Come sit by me and tell me all about yourself."

I place my purse on a chair and sit in the one next to him.

"Did you and my son date in high school?"

"No, he dated my friend Jackie, though. Did you meet her?"

George frowns and looks over at his son. "Don't think I ever did. Who's Jackie?"

Bobby sighs. "You met her once or twice."

George frowns and peers up at the ceiling as if he's searching his memory. "Curly, black hair, blue eyes?"

Bobby nods.

"Now I remember. Quiet little thing. Used to slip into your room without saying hello. I could never maneuver this chair fast enough to intercept her to chat."

"Jackie was shy." So he's been in the wheelchair for a long time then. An injury? Sickness? I don't remember ever seeing him at any of Bobby's games in high school. But then, my parents never came to watch me cheer either.

Bobby brings the paperwork back to the receptionist, and she gives him a wide smile. Yeah, she's interested. Has he dated her?

"Tell me about you, Lucinda. What do you do?"

I smile at George. "I've recently reinvented myself as a wedding planner."

"That sounds like a fun job. I imagine you have to be detail-oriented to do a job like that."

"Yes, you do. I enjoy it."

"Bobby here is detail-oriented too. Has to be to run his business and keep all his employees, clients, and equipment straight all the time. I don't know how he does it. I'm not about the details like he is. I'm more of a 'see where the wind takes me' type of person." He shrugs with a smile. "Has its upsides and downsides like anything else."

Bobby has employees? I only ever see him working on his own.

"He keeps track of everything on the computer. Turned his old bedroom into his office and uses the smaller spare bedroom

for sleeping. He just bought another truck and trailer. He's got
—" He looks at Bobby. "How many employees you got now,
son?"

"Six." Bobby stares out the window and drums his fingers on
his legs.

So he still lives at home with his father. To help take care of
him? Bobby said his mother took off when he was young. That's
a lot to take on as a kid. I glance at Bobby. How would I have
handled all that at his age? Probably not well.

"That's right, six now. He started the business from nothing
and now has a fleet of trucks."

"Three trucks are hardly a fleet." Bobby tilts his head back
and closes his eyes.

I smile at George. "That's quite impressive." He's obviously
very proud of his son and his accomplishments. I wish my
parents felt the same about me. They had seemed proud when I
became a lawyer like my father. Now, not so much.

"You should see the gardens he designed for this rich couple
on the lake. It's an old estate and has a maze and everything."

"Pops, Lucinda is Franny's sister. She's seen the estate. How
about you tell her about your birdhouses?" Bobby shifts in his
chair and glances between me and his father. "He designs and
builds birdhouses. Sells them on the internet. In fact, Franny
and Mitch just commissioned him to make a miniature version
of their house for one. Isn't that right, Pops?"

"You're Franny's sister? She makes the most amazing
desserts. Bobby brings me a box from her bakery every once in
a while. I've only talked to her on the phone twice. She's real
sweet."

"She is, and she does make wonderful treats. I rent the apartment over her bakery and sneak a treat or two too many times."
I touch the top of his hand. "I'd love to see your birdhouses. I'm
not artistic or crafty. It always amazes me when someone can
create something from nothing with their hands."

"Then you'll have to come by the house sometime. You can come over for dinner." He glances sideways at Bobby. "Wouldn't that be nice to have Lucinda over for dinner?"

Oh boy, I'm not sure our truce can extend that far. He may have let his image of me from high school go, but I'm not sure he wants to become friends, either. And certainly not the date his father appears to be pushing for.

"I think you should have her over for lunch sometime so she can see your birdhouses in the sunlight."

"Doesn't get dark until later—"

"Mr. Calvert, Dr. Fox will see you now." A nurse in blue scrubs with flowers on the top stands in an open doorway.

Bobby stands.

"Sit down and keep Lucinda company. Doctors make her nervous. I can handle this visit on my own." George turns his head and smiles at me. "Lucinda, I hope to see you again real soon."

"It was nice meeting you, George."

He wheels across the room. I turn to Bobby, who's still standing watching his father. "You don't need to keep me company. I'm fine."

He glances at me and sits down. "Why do doctors make you nervous?"

"When I was a kid, my dentist used to swear and mumble under his breath at me and throw things. Didn't exactly alleviate the fears I already had." I shrug. "It's not exactly rational, but every time I have to go see a medical professional, I get anxious. My mother used to get so angry with me for embarrassing her."

"Your mother's default setting seems to be anger."

I smile. "True."

"Listen, Pops likes to talk. Don't feel obligated to come see his birdhouses. I know you were just being polite. I'll make an excuse for you."

"What happened to our truce?"

He looks at me with one eyebrow raised.

"I thought you were going to stop making judgements about me based on the past or hearsay. I like your father and would love to see his birdhouses. But I get you don't want me showing up for dinner or anything. I'll visit him sometime when you're at work."

"Fair enough."

The door opens and a different nurse in pink scrubs walks into the waiting room. "Lucinda Dawson?" Why do I still get that tiny hitch in my shoulders when anyone uses my maiden name? I haven't used Mark's since I moved back to Granite Cove.

I smile at the nurse and stand before looking at Bobby. "I'll get your father's phone number from Franny." She'll have it because of the birdhouse she ordered and that way I won't have to deal with Bobby as a middleman since he obviously doesn't want our truce to extend to actual friendship.

CHAPTER 9

$\mathcal{T}$he radio hosts bicker over politics, so I shut off the car radio. I'll be turning onto my parents' street in a minute, anyway. I stop at the stop sign and tap my fingers along the sides of the steering wheel.

Tina's baby shower went perfectly. I couldn't have asked for anything better. Tina was thrilled and glowing the entire time. Her family and coworkers all seemed to have a fun time. Another successfully planned event under my belt. Even if it wasn't a paid event, it was still experience and a success. Besides, a well-executed party for a friend is more important. We'll have to start planning Kelly's baby shower next.

Bobby stands next to his truck at my parents' house. I could drive by and come back another time. I did as he asked and visited his father when he wasn't there last week. I wish I had a place to hang a birdhouse. I thought of ordering one for Father's Day, but there wouldn't have been enough time and Mother probably would've refused to have it in her yard, anyway. Dad was happy with the new golf outfit I gave him at brunch on Sunday.

No, it would be ridiculous to drive by because he's there. I already forgot to pick up my box of stuff last time because I ended up fighting with my mother. I need to search through my old sketches of wedding ideas. I pull into their driveway and park.

Bobby nods once in my direction when I get out of the car and wave. I suppose a nod is a step up from the ignoring or shunning he used to treat me to.

Mother's tremulous raised voice sounds from the kitchen, "Grant?"

So much for my hope no one would be home and I could sneak in and out without another confrontation. I open my mouth to tell her it's me and not my father, but her voice sounds again before I can.

"Grant!"

She almost sounds...afraid. I push open the kitchen door. Mother stands by the counter clutching her throat. Her gaze swings to me and then to the floor.

I follow her gaze and gasp. Dad is on the floor unconscious. My entire body freezes, and it feels like my breath is locked inside my chest. My eyes sting.

A surge of adrenaline rockets through me. "Dad!" I drop to my knees next to him. "What happened?"

My mother shakes her head and backs up a step. "I...he..." She shakes her head again.

Ice forms in my stomach. What do I do? I grab my phone from my pocket and dial nine-one-one as I feel for a pulse and check if he's breathing. *Oh God! Please, please let him be okay!*

A dispatcher answers. "What is your emergency?"

Is that his pulse? Why can't I feel his breath?

"It's my father. He's unconscious. I don't know what happened. I found him this way." I rattle off their address.

"Mother!"

Her wild gaze lands on me.

"What happened? They need to know!"

"His chest. He...he...clutched his chest."

I drop my phone on the floor and put it on speaker so I can talk and do CPR at the same time. The dispatcher's calm voice drones on with instructions and questions. I do chest compressions and rescue breaths, staring at his face and chest for any sign they're working. Am I doing it right? It's been years since I took a first aid course. What's the ratio of compressions and breaths? Thirty and two? *Damn it! I lost count!*

Bobby bursts into the kitchen and drops next to me. "What can I do?"

"I...I don't know." My gaze darts between my father's face and chest. My heartbeat thunders in my ears. A numbness spreads through my limbs.

"Here, I'll take over." His hands slide under mine and he starts the compressions.

I drop back on my knees and stare at my father. Is he already gone?

A shrill siren shrieks closer and closer to the house. *Thank God!* The ambulance.

I climb to my feet and stumble out the kitchen door. The front door is already open. Bobby must have left it open when he came inside.

"He's in the kitchen."

An emergency person brushes past me. I follow him back. He takes over for Bobby. I stand with my arms folded around my middle. What should I do?

More people file in and work on my father.

Someone says they have a pulse. I sag against the cabinet behind me. Does that mean he'll be okay?

They move him to a gurney and wheel him out.

We trail behind them as they load him into the ambulance. An officer talks to my mother and walks with her to the ambulance. She climbs into the front of the ambulance.

"I'll take you to the hospital."

"What?" I turn and my surroundings blur.

An arm slides around my shoulders. "Come on. Adrenaline is wearing off."

My hands shake as Bobby helps me into his truck like I'm a child. I should protest and tell him I'm fine, but the words won't come.

What if he dies?

Bobby makes a U-turn. "We're only five minutes from the hospital here. He's got a good chance."

I scrub the tears off my cheeks and stare at some crumbled papers on the floor of his truck. Yes, Churchill Memorial is close. But he was so pale, and why didn't he wake up? I rub my arms together. They're sore. Did I not do the compressions right? Was I not strong enough?

"She just stood there."

"What?" I feel Bobby's glance.

"My mother. She just stood there. How long was he on the floor before I came in? Why wasn't she doing anything? Calling nine-one-one?"

"Shock probably. He was still alive. That's a good sign."

Is it? Of course it is. It's better than the alternative.

I scrub my face hard and sniffle. "How did you know?"

"I heard you scream at your mother."

Did I? I guess I must have.

Tears continue to fill my eyes and overflow down my cheeks. Sobs shudder through me. I gulp for air. My father might die. He might already be gone.

Bobby turns into the hospital parking lot and parks.

He pulls me into his arms and rubs my back. "Breathe."

I fist my fingers into his T-shirt and sob against his chest.

What are we going to do if he dies?

I suck in a breath. *Franny!* I have to call Franny. I search my pockets for my phone.

"What is it?"

"My phone. I left it at the house. I have to call Franny."

"Here." He slides my phone out of his pocket. "I picked it up."

"Thank you." I open my phone. "Thank you for everything." I stare at him. "I don't know what we would've done."

"You were already handling it."

I pull up Franny's number. Her smiling face stares back at me and tears fill my eyes once again.

"She's in California with Mitch visiting his parents. Should I not call?"

"Would you want to know if the situation was reversed?"

I nod. What am I going to say to her? How do I tell her?

"Maybe I should get more information first." I look up at the hospital and grab the door handle. "I should go inside. Thank you for everything. I'm okay now."

He climbs out of his truck. "I'm not leaving you alone to deal with this."

I should tell him to go. It's not his problem. I'm not his problem. My lips quiver and I twist them and press them between my teeth.

He takes my arm and I follow him inside.

CHAPTER 10

"It sounds stupid, but I never considered the possibility of my father dying one day. I mean, I realize my parents aren't immortal or impervious to harm."

"Yeah, it can be a punch to the gut when you realize how fast life can change."

I suck in a breath and put my hand on Bobby's arm. "I'm sorry. That was insensitive of me."

He frowns. "Why?"

"Your father is in a wheelchair and your mother is gone. Of course you understand more than most about how fragile parents can be."

He looks down the hall of the hospital.

I rub my cheeks and gaze around at the nurses hustling by. My mother sits across from me. Every few minutes she'll rise, clutch her throat, and pace the waiting room. She's barely spoken a dozen words to me. At least she's communicating with the doctors and nurses.

The ICU waiting room is much bigger than the tiny, family, emergency waiting room they stuffed us into when we first arrived. The four rows of blue cushioned chairs are empty except for us.

"It was a boat accident. My father."

"Oh."

"He was paralyzed from the waist down. He was lucky. The other guy died. My mother took off while he was still in the hospital." He looks around. "It hasn't changed much since then. Same generic pictures on the wall."

"I'm sorry, Bobby. I didn't realize. You've been here for hours with me. This must be difficult for you. You can go. I'll be fine, really. Franny is on her way." I glance at the clock. "They should actually be here in a little while since Mitch chartered a private jet to get them here quicker."

He shakes his head. "I'm fine. They're just memories. It was a long time ago. I was ten. I'll stay until they get here."

Ten? He was only ten when he almost lost his father and his mother abandoned him?

"My grandparents, Pop's parents, stepped in and took care of us. They helped as much as they could until they both got sick and passed away within a few months of each other my senior year of high school."

"I'm so sorry. I don't know what to say."

"Nothing to say. I guess I'm just stuck in the memories." He looks around. "Can I get you anything?"

I glance over at my mother. "You should eat something."

She doesn't spare either of us a glance. She just shakes her head.

"I'll go find something for us to drink." Bobby walks down the hall and I scoot over to the chair next to my mother.

I take her hand, but she pulls away. That's the second time she's done that today. She's never been the most affectionate woman, but I'm trying to offer her comfort. It would be nice if she could at least be receptive. It's not only her husband but my father who we're waiting to hear news about.

I sigh and rub my forehead. "Is there anything I can do for you?"

"You could tell the gardener to go. This time is for family. What is your relationship with that man, anyway?"

I squeeze my eyes closed and count to ten in my head. "That man helped save your husband. He happens to be kind and decent, and I consider him my friend."

I do now anyway.

She shoots me a glare before rising and walking over to the window on the other side of the room. I slide back to the chair I was sitting in before I got the useless notion to try to comfort my mother again. Why do I bother?

I tilt my head back against the wall and stare at the square white tiles on the ceiling. You'd think the icy heart inside her would've melted just a little. Shouldn't she be grateful Bobby tried to save Dad? She certainly did nothing.

I wince and squeeze my eyes closed. That's not fair. She was in shock and panicking. It's not like she did nothing on purpose. I look over at her staring out the window.

No, not even my mother is that cold.

Is she?

I shake my head. I can't go there. Mother is a lot of things, but she's not a murderer. Dad had a heart attack, and she panicked.

God! How can I be sitting here considering this?

A coffee dangles in front of me. "Here, there's not much of a selection." Bobby glances over at my mother. "Should I bring this over to her?" He tilts the other coffee in his hand.

I take one coffee and shake my head. "I wouldn't. She's in a mood."

He shrugs and sits next to me. "Any word?"

I shake my head.

A doctor in blue scrubs walks into the waiting room. My

mother whirls from the window and strides across to meet him. I jump up from my chair.

The doctor murmurs to my mother and she clasps her hand over her mouth and nods. I jog over.

"He's in recovery. You can see him in a few minutes." He looks at me. "One at a time."

"He's going to be okay?"

"Everything looks promising. He has a hard road ahead of him, but I expect him to make a full recovery. The nurse will bring you in to see him shortly."

I sag over my knees. *He's going to be okay.*

Bobby squeezes my hand when I stand up straight. I squeeze his hand back and grin. "He's going to be okay."

He smiles and nods.

I turn to my mother with a smile. She lifts her chin and crosses her arms over her waist. "I'll go in first."

"Of course."

The nurse comes and escorts my mother down the hall. I pace the waiting room.

I'll have good news to share with Franny when she arrives. I was so scared it wouldn't be.

Bobby walks over and hands me the coffee I left on the table by the chair.

"Thanks."

I glance at the clock. "I'm just going to peek in at him. The doctor said one at a time, but I just need to see him."

Bobby nods and takes the coffee back out of my hands. "Go."

The nurse that escorted my mother walks out of a room. I wait until she goes to the nursing station, then stride down to the room and peek in.

Dad lies on the bed covered in a green blanket. His eyes are closed and there's a clear mask over his nose and mouth. A machine beeps. He's so pale and still.

My mother's head rests on his stomach. Her shoulders shake. Sobs drift out the door.

Tears fill my eyes and I rest my head against the wall. So she does care.

CHAPTER 11

$\mathcal{T}$he black and pink box from The Sweet Spot shifts on the passenger seat as I go around a corner. I bought all the raspberry turnovers, Bobby's favorite, and I had Franny add an assortment of treats for George, too. I meant to drop by his house sooner, but with all the back-and-forth visits to the hospital, the days sort of melted together. But Dad is home now and settled in with Mother doting on him.

She barely tolerates Franny and my presence when we visit. She insists we're going to tire him out. I suppose I should be thankful she's taking such good care of him.

Bobby might not appreciate me dropping by like this, but I have to find some way to thank him for helping with Dad and staying with me at the hospital. He hasn't been doing the landscaping at my parents' house any of the times I've visited Dad. I figured I would've bumped into him there at least once in the past couple of weeks.

He disappeared when Rebecca and Olivia showed up. I still can't believe he thought of calling them. It never even occurred to me. But they were wonderful and I'm so glad they were there, especially once Franny arrived and we turned into blubbering messes.

The small brown ranch with the large garage on the side comes into view. The large, verdant, green lawn has perfectly uniform diagonal rows. I guess it would be poor advertising for a landscaper to have a brown, patchy lawn. When I visited George last time, he once again raved about Bobby's business and told me how Bobby built the garage a few years ago when he expanded his business. It's easily twice the size of the house. There's a ramp and workshop on the back for George to build his beautiful birdhouses.

Bobby stands on the walkway talking to a blonde woman. Well, at least I know he's home. If he's busy, I'll just visit with George.

As soon as I park, Bobby opens my door and grabs my hand. "My girlfriend and I have plans. You have to go."

Okay, then why are you dragging me out of my car? I glance at the woman. This is his girlfriend? She's certainly attractive, but she's got to be at least fifty.

Bobby puts his arm around my shoulders.

I look between him and his girlfriend. What is he doing?

She holds out her hand. "It's so nice to meet you. I'm Peyton, Bobby's mother."

My mouth drops open. Not his girlfriend. His mother. I shake her hand and force a smile to my lips. "I'm Lucinda." And apparently Bobby's girlfriend.

I drop her hand. His mother is back? And he wants to use me to get rid of her? Okay, it's the least I can do.

"I'm so sorry we have to run, but Bobby promised to help me with …um, moving some furniture. My father just came home from the hospital and we need to make room for special equipment." She doesn't need to know he's been home for a couple of weeks.

"I hope your father is okay, Lucinda." Peyton looks between Bobby and me. "You make such a beautiful couple."

Bobby stands rigidly beside me and doesn't say a word. I wrap my arm around his waist and smile. "Thank you. He's doing much better. But we really should be going."

"Of course." She looks at Bobby and then back at the house. "I'll be in touch." She walks over to a red sedan parked on the other side of my car.

Bobby remains silent as she backs out of the driveway. I lift my hand and wave when she glances over her shoulder at us.

He drops his arm from my shoulders when her car disappears from view.

"You realize she's going to come back, right?"

He scrubs his hands over his face. "Yeah, but maybe I'll have some time to prepare for it."

"She just showed up without warning?"

He nods and puts his hands on his hips. "Thanks for playing along."

"Sure, happy to help. If it actually helped." I glance down the road. "What are you going to do?"

"Not a clue. I guess find out what the hell she wants while making sure she leaves my father the hell alone."

"Where is George?"

"At the senior center. He goes there to play bridge once a week."

"You don't want him to know about her?"

His head swings around and he pins me with his gaze. "Hell no! And don't you dare tell him."

"That's certainly not my place and I wouldn't, but don't you think you should warn him? What if she shows up at the door when you're not home? You want time to prepare. He probably would too."

"Shit!" He stares up at the sky.

"I don't want her anywhere near him. It took years for him

76

to climb out of the depression the accident and her leaving left him in."

George depressed? But he's so playful and charming.

"What can I do?"

He glances at me and shakes his head. "I could send Pops on a vacation. Get Carrie, his nurse, to go with him for assistance in case he needs it."

"How feasible is that? I don't know Carrie, but can she just drop everything to go away with your father? And will George be willing to go without an explanation?"

He throws his hands up in the air. "He hates traveling. Won't get on a plane. The farthest I've ever gotten him to go in a car is Boston for a doctor appointment, and I had to nag him for months for that to happen."

"Then I doubt the vacation idea is going to work."

He stares at me with a look of desperation on his face. "What am I going to do?"

"Does your mother have any friends or relatives still in town or nearby?"

"Not that I'm aware of. She doesn't have any family, at least none that I've ever heard of."

"Then if she's staying in town, there are only a few options: White Birch Inn, a rental, Rosewood Bed & Breakfast, and I think there's one other B&B."

He nods. "You're right. I'll find out where she's staying, find out what she wants, and get rid of her before Pops finds out." He sighs heavily. "I should've just found out while she was here, but I was worried Pops would come home and see her here."

"Understandable. It must have been pretty jarring for you to have her show up out of the blue. Are you okay?"

Bobby stares past me into my car. "What's in the box?"

"Oh, that's a thank-you for all your help. I know raspberry turnovers are your favorite." I guess he doesn't want to talk about how his mother's return affects him.

"They are. What'd you do, buy out the entire case?"

"I added some treats for your father, too." I walk around and get the box from the passenger side.

"Want to take those inside and share? You can help me call around and figure out where she is."

"Sure."

What could his mother possibly want? To reconnect? Apologize for abandoning him and his father when they needed her most?

We walk up the ramp to the house. He holds the door open. "Listen, I'd appreciate it if you kept this to yourself. I don't want people gossiping and it getting back to Pops."

"I don't gossip. Well, not about anything that's supposed to be kept private." I walk past him into the house. "I won't say a word. Not even to Franny."

"Thanks."

CHAPTER 12

"*H*ey, fake boyfriend."

Bobby looks over his shoulder and chuckles. "Hey."

I admire the view of him bent over, fiddling with the equipment on his trailer as I walk over. My fake boyfriend certainly has a nice physique.

He stands and brushes off his hands.

"It's funny. When I was looking for you the past couple of weeks while I was visiting Dad, you were never here, so I had to show up at your house. Now of course, you're here again."

He snorts. "Yeah well, blame your mother for that one. She fired me right after the hospital. Your father hired me back yesterday."

"Again? I'm so sorry."

"Why are you sorry? You're not responsible for your mother's actions."

"Still. Why do you put up with it? Why come back?"

"Because your father gave me a thousand bucks back when I was first starting my business. It allowed me to buy some used equipment. I paid him back years ago, of course. I tried to pay him interest too, but he wouldn't take it." He shrugs. "I owe him, and putting up with your mother is a small price to pay."

"I had no idea. He never said a word." I glance at the house. "Mother actually called me and asked me to come over and sit with Dad while she goes out to run some errands. Considering she's barely been speaking to me, I was surprised." I touch his arm. "Oh, speaking of mothers, did you talk to yours?"

"Yeah, I went to the B&B last night." He folds his arms over his chest and stares down the road. "She wanted money. Gave me a sad spiel about how she married too young and felt trapped. She said she never got her fair share of the house or a divorce settlement." He shakes his head. "She went on and on about the hard life she's lived and how Pops owes her."

"Please tell me you didn't give her any money."

"Hell no! I told her we mortgaged the house to the hilt to pay medical bills, and she's not getting a dime. Then I said if she didn't get out of town and stay away from Pops, I would see she was sued for back child support, skipping out on the bills, and anything else I could think of. I certainly wasn't going to tell her I paid all that off years ago. The house isn't in her name and never was. It was Pop's before they married."

"Good for you. Do you think it'll work?"

"She left town. The B&B called me this morning. She skipped out on her bill and left a note saying I'd be responsible for payment. I paid it but made it clear if she came back, I wasn't paying for anything."

"She's unbelievable!"

Bobby shrugs. "It is what it is. I better get to work, and your mother is peeking out the window."

I whirl around as the curtain in the living room drops back into place.

"See you later, Bobby."

"See you."

The door opens before I set foot on the steps. She didn't say the errands were urgent. Why is she in such a hurry?

Silly question. It's my mother. When she wants something, everyone is supposed to jump to attention immediately.

"Really, Lucinda, you could have made yourself more presentable."

I glance down at my white shorts and blue T-shirt. "I didn't realize keeping Dad company required me to dress up."

"You don't even have any makeup on."

I skipped book club for this? "Actually I'm wearing mascara."

"Come upstairs with me and I'll find something for you to wear and fix your face. Quickly—"

"Hi, baby."

Every cell in my body locks in place. Mark appears in the archway to the living room. He walks over and leans down to kiss me.

I stumble backwards and bump into the railing of the stairs. *What is he doing here?*

"When your mother called and invited me for a visit, I was thrilled. I've missed you."

I glare at my mother. She called and invited my ex-husband for a visit?

She wrings her hands and lifts her chin. "Yes, you're spiraling out of control, Lucinda. You're making horrible decisions with your life. Mark was a good, steadying influence on you. You were good together. You both made mistakes. It's time to grow up and accept responsibility."

She called my ex-husband. My serial cheating ex-husband.

I've made mistakes? What the hell mistake did I make up besides staying with him for so long?

She squirms under my glare. Good. You better squirm, Mother. You better pray I don't give in to my desire to strangle you with my bare hands!

Mark rubs a hand down my arm and my skin crawls. I yank my arm away and turn my glare on him.

"You've made a mistake. There's nothing here for you. She never should have called you. We're divorced."

"You know I never wanted a divorce, baby. Let's go somewhere and talk."

Right, you wanted us to have an open marriage so you could go on sleeping with anyone you wanted and use me as the excuse to get rid of them.

I catch my mother's smile out of the corner of my eye and turn my glare back at her. Pure ice spreads through my veins—like a deep blue glacier that's been submerged under water for decades and suddenly breaks free and bursts to the surface.

"Mark, go back in the living room, please. I need to speak to my mother for a moment."

"Sure, baby."

Mother steps closer and whispers furiously, "Don't blow this opportunity! He wants you back."

"You've gone too far, Mother."

"What was I supposed to do? Watch you squander your life away in this town planning other brides' weddings? You're almost thirty! Your youth is dwindling away! You should thank me for calling Mark."

"You'd rather see me with a man who valued our marriage so little he cheated on me repeatedly than be happy doing something I love?"

She waves her hand as if everything I've said is inconsequential. "Men have dalliances. Don't be so damn naïve. You think your father never strayed? As long as he comes home to you and doesn't keep any of them for long, they're not a threat. And if they become one, there are ways to handle that too."

Who is this woman? Who are my parents?

My father cheated? She doesn't care?

"We're done, Mother. You've finally gone too far. Stay the

hell out of my life!"

She grabs hold of my arm in a death grip. Her manicured talons dig into my skin. "You will stop these hysterics and march into the living room and smile. You will flirt and let Mark woo you back."

"You are insane!"

"Your looks aren't going to last much longer. They're already fading. Why do you think you're alone? Where are all the men? Do you see them lining up at your door?"

The whine of a motor sounds outside the house. *Bobby.*

"I have a boyfriend, Mother."

I turn and slam open the front door. Bobby stands in front of the dining room windows holding a machine. He's wearing goggles and grass clippings are flying in every direction. He looks up as I stomp down the stairs.

The machine stops when he flicks a switch and frowns in my direction.

"Lucinda! Get back in this house!" Mother stands on the steps, pointing back inside. Mark stands behind her.

"I told you, Mother. I have a boyfriend."

I fist my hands in Bobby's T-shirt, yank him down to me, and plant a kiss on his lips.

Not daring to look at his face, I put my arm around his waist and face my mother and Mark, who both stand on the steps.

Bobby puts his arm over my shoulders.

My mother snarls, "You're fired," at Bobby and stalks into the house and slams the door.

Mark gazes at Bobby and then at me. "I'll be staying at the inn in town for a few days, baby. We should have dinner." He walks over to a black sedan parked on the street in front of Bobby's truck.

"Have you lost your mind?" Bobby drops his arm from my shoulders.

Probably.

CHAPTER 13

*R*ebecca opens the door with a smile, which fades immediately when she looks at my face. "What's wrong?"

I walk past her into her house, toe off my sandals, and pad straight to the pool table in front of me. Murmurs of conversation from the book club ladies come from my left. I climb onto the pool table and lie down, staring up at the ceiling.

Rebecca stops next to me.

"Is this okay? I can move if you want. I think." I fold my hands over my abdomen and flick my nails together.

"Honey, you can lie down anywhere you want." She pats me on the shoulder. "What happened?"

"Luce? What's going on? Are you sick?" Franny puts her hand on my forehead.

I shake my head slowly.

"What can I do?" Franny takes my hand.

"Anyone got any smelling salts, like in the book? You know, like the ones Elizabeth carried around for all her daft cousins?" I angle my head toward Franny. "Don't you wish we had cousins growing up? Not like Elizabeth's obviously; they were awful."

Franny looks over my head at the ladies who've circled around the table. "Uh, I don't think I've ever really contemplated it, Luce."

"Do they even make smelling salts anymore? Someone should look that up. I'd do it, but I don't remember where I left my phone." I pat my thighs. "Nope, no pockets."

"Is she drunk?"

I roll my eyes back toward Kelly. "Nope, I haven't had a drop. Sounds like an excellent idea, though. Where's the wine? And a straw, please. I'm not sure I can sit up right now."

Monica pats my other hand. "I'll get you some as soon as we're sure you're not having some sort of medical emergency."

"Not unless you count insanity. They used the smelling salts when people fainted. They were meant to shock the women awake, right? My brain needs a kick start. It might be in shock."

"Says here, smelling salts were made with ammonia." Olivia shows the group her phone screen.

I wrinkle my nose. "I think that would just make me gag." I close my eyes and lay my arm over them.

"Talk to us, Luce. Let us help you." Franny squeezes my hand.

"Mother called and said she needed me to stay with Dad while she ran errands."

"Okay, so this has to do with her?" Franny sighs. "What's she done now? Here I believed she was relatively pleasant since Dad's heart attack. Wait, Dad's okay, isn't he?"

"As far as I know, he's fine. He's a cheater, but fine."

Franny sucks in a breath. "What?"

I lower my arm and wince. "Oh my God, I'm sorry. I shouldn't have said it like that." Crap, I'm awful.

Franny fingers her necklace and frowns down at me. "Luce, tell me what's going on. Are you saying Dad is cheating?"

"No, I mean not that I know of. Currently. But according to

Mother, he has in the past. She dropped that little bombshell while she was insisting I give Mark another chance."

"Mark? She started talking about Mark?"

"Oh, didn't I mention she called me over because Mark was there?"

"No, you didn't mention that little tidbit." Rebecca folds her arms. "Why was your ex-husband at your parents' house?"

"Because she called him and told him what a mess I was without him and he needed to come rescue me."

"You've got to be blankety-blank kidding me!"

We all turn and stare at Olivia.

She shrugs and winces. "Swear jar is working."

I look at Franny. "I'm done with her this time. This is it. I told her so too."

Franny nods, climbs onto the table next to me, and lies down. "I'm done too. I'd say I can't believe she did that, but I really can."

"I'll get you that wine now." Monica walks toward the kitchen.

Franny stares at me. "How are you laying here? This table is really uncomfortable."

I smile. She's right, it is. It's worse than the floor.

Rebecca chuckles. "It's not exactly meant for people to lie on."

I lift my arms. "Pull me up please."

Rebecca and Olivia grab my hands and pull.

Franny sits up next to me. "Can we relocate to the couches now?"

"Yes, my dramatic moment has passed—mostly."

Once we all move to the living room, Monica hands me a glass of wine. "So you told your mother you're done with her. What did you say to your ex? Did he really believe if he showed up, you'd fall back into his arms after everything he's done and all this time?"

"He sure did."

"He must have an enormous ego. It's been what, two years?" Kelly positions herself in the couch's corner with a pillow propped on either side of her.

Franny laughs. "Oh, he's got an ego all right. Talk to him for a minute and he'll tell you how wonderful he is."

Rebecca crosses her legs and swings her foot. "He's one of those, is he? I always think they must be overcompensating for something."

Chuckles circle the room.

"Well Lucinda? Is he overcompensating?"

I glance at Kelly. "If you're asking about his penis size, I'd say he's average." I drop my head to the back of the couch. "He's had no trouble getting women though, even during our marriage. He's staying at the inn for a few days and wants to have dinner. That will not happen." I lift my head. "Did I mention I told Mother and Mark Bobby is my boyfriend and marched outside and kissed him?"

"Uh no."

"You definitely left that part out."

"Excuse me now?"

I laugh so hard the wine in my glass sloshes back and forth. I take a deep gulp. I have to save Rebecca's furniture, after all.

Olivia scoots forward. "How did Bobby react?"

"Thankfully, he didn't shove me away or anything. He put his arm around me and stood rigidly next to me until they both left. Then he asked me if I was crazy."

I'd gotten in my car and left shortly after. How I made it here alive and without getting in an accident is a miracle. I must've driven on autopilot.

"At least I didn't have to miss book club after all." I raise my glass.

∾

"LUCE! WAIT UP."

I stop at my car door and wait for Franny to catch up. "If you're worried about my driving, I'll be fine. I only had the one glass, and that was a while ago. I ate plenty to soak any wine up."

"No, that's not it." She frowns and looks over her shoulder.

Everyone else is still inside except for Kelly; she already left.

"How close are you getting with Bobby?"

"Franny, we're just friends. I panicked. I just wanted to shut Mom up and make Mark go away."

"It's just that you two seem to hang around together a lot."

"I wouldn't say a lot. It's just coincidence, mostly. Is there some reason you don't want me to be friends with Bobby? I thought you liked him."

"I do. It's not that."

"Then what is it?"

"I'm not sure if I should tell you this or not, but you're my sister and…"

"Franny, you're freaking me out a bit here. I've had enough shocks to my system today. Just spit it out."

She huffs out a big puff of air. "Okay. You remember my friend, Mrs. Roberts?"

"The elderly lady who lives up the street from the bakery? The one you bring treats to, right?"

"Yes. She told me something once that has to do with Bobby's parents. I'm not sure how true it is or anything. I just know what she said."

"And that is?"

"There was a boat accident."

"Yes, I know. George, Bobby's dad, was injured in it. That's why he's in a wheelchair. Why his mother took off."

"Yes. Did Bobby talk to you about it?"

"Only a little bit, why?"

"Did he tell you someone was killed in the accident?"

"Yes, he said his father was lucky because there was another man who didn't make it."

"And that's it?"

"Yes. Franny, what's going on?"

"The other man was Charlie Roberts. Mrs. Roberts' husband. He was having an affair with Bobby's mother."

"Oh."

That doesn't surprise me too much. The woman is awful.

"Charlie Roberts was a horrible man. He had a lot of women, but that's not all. He was a thief. He spent years in prison for it."

"Then it sounds like Peyton and him were made for each other."

"Peyton?"

"Bobby's mother."

"Mrs. Roberts said Bobby's mother disappeared."

"She did. She abandoned Bobby and his father after the accident." I promised not to tell anyone, including Franny, about Peyton showing up. Crap!

Franny bites her lip and puts her hand on my arm. "Luce, Mrs. Roberts said she didn't have proof, but she concluded Bobby's parents might've murdered Charlie."

I suck in a breath. Speech deserts me. Murdered? By Bobby's parents?

Peyton maybe. But not George.

"Wasn't the accident investigated?"

"All I know is what she told me. She seemed pretty confident. She only told me because she believed I was dating Bobby and she wanted to warn me." She fingers the tiny cross on her necklace. "Ever since Bobby started working for us, I've wanted to tell him, but I'm not sure what the right thing to do is. Mrs. Roberts might be way off base. It might've just been an accident. I certainly don't want to be the one to tell Bobby she accused his parents of murder."

"So you think I should? He only recently started speaking to me. I doubt he'd want to hear it from me."

"But you believe he should know?"

I lift my shoulders and purse my lips. "If it was our parents, would you want to be told?"

"I'm not sure. I'm still reeling from the news Dad cheated."

"I know. She just stated it like it was no big deal." I rub my forehead. "I've got to think on this. It's been a hell of a day."

"Okay. Sorry, I just thought you should know. And, well, I guess I didn't want to be the only one with this information. It's been nagging at me." Franny gives me a hug. "Call me if you need me. If Mark darkens your door, I'll chase him off with one of my marble rolling pins."

I chuckle as the image of Franny chasing Mark with a rolling pin flashes in my head. "Thanks."

CHAPTER 14

The dark gray decking spans the width of the back of the building. Thirty feet of wide open space. The crew Franny hired really did a wonderful job. I haven't yet purchased any outdoor furniture for the space. The wrap-around couch and umbrella I've got pinned to my decorating boards on Pinterest are a tad bit out of my budget at the moment.

Voices drift up from the patio below. Customers seem to love the expanded seating Franny added to the bakery. Who wouldn't enjoy sitting and enjoying the lake view while munching on Franny's exquisite desserts?

Thankfully, the way the deck and patio are designed, I still have my privacy. It's only a quiet murmur up here and they can't see me. I'd have to lean over the railing to see any customers. Of course, they can probably hear me pacing back and forth or see the shadow of me between the deck boards.

I lean against the railing facing the parking lot behind the docks and Billings Creamery. What am I going to do about Bobby and the information about his parents? I wish Franny never told me. I drop my head down to the railing. Now that I know, I can't erase it. I can't ignore it. There's a reason there's a saying to not kill the messenger. People tend to blame the person who delivers the message along with the ones who are actually responsible.

Bobby may very well hate me if I tell him. He'll go back to giving me the cold shoulder and ignoring my existence. Or he'll make snide comments and make me feel like pond scum. It's not like there is any evidence. It's only speculation. Do I really have to tell him someone mentioned Charlie Roberts' death might not have been an accident? That the boat explosion that almost killed his father might've been intentional, and his parents might've had something to do with it?

What will it change? Will it damage his relationship with his father? His relationship with his mother is already damaged. She left town. Maybe I should keep silent.

I raise my head and stare at the blue sky overhead. There's not a cloud in sight. The breeze off the lake ruffles my hair against my neck. Would I want to be told if it were my parents, even if it was only speculation?

Damn it! Yes, I would. I'd want all the facts so I could make my own informed decision. I wouldn't want someone to keep information from me. But will Bobby feel the same way?

The bottom ruffled edges of the red and white awnings at Billings Creamery flutter from the wind. Boats bob against the town docks. A familiar truck backs down the boat ramp with an empty trailer. Bobby must've spent the morning fishing.

I briefly glare up at the sky. Trying to send me a sign? I sigh and jog down the steps. Far be it from me to ignore the universe telling me to do the right thing, even though it might blow up in my face.

They split the stairs against the side of the patio to provide a barrier from the parking lot and to give me some privacy while coming and going. I glance at the back door of the bakery at the bottom of the stairs. It'd be nice to have Franny for backup, but

I can tell by the number of customers on the patio that she'll be busy. The windows reflect the view of the lake instead of allowing customers to see in the bakery's kitchen. They highlight the view and allow Franny to keep her privacy. The row of tall potted bushes lining my stairs and the walkway to the back door also helps.

I look back toward the boat ramp. The view isn't as clear from down here. What if he's already loaded his boat and left?

Then I'll take that as another sign to wait.

My steps might be a little slower than they could be as I cross the parking lot. It's not like I'm actually dragging my feet in the hope he'll be gone by the time I get there, but I'm not rushing either.

The front of his truck comes into view and I grimace. Okay, okay, time to spill the beans.

Bobby cranks a lever at the front of his trailer and tosses something into the back of his truck as I walk down the ramp. There are a handful of vehicles with empty trailers parked along the side.

"Catch anything?"

He glances over his shoulder and the corner of his mouth lifts in a smile. "Hey."

I'm really going to miss him smiling at me instead of scowling.

He tilts his head toward the boat and lake. "I caught a few."

"So it's fish for dinner?"

"No, I let them all go." He shrugs. "I've always been more of a fan of the catching part than the cleaning and cooking part."

I tuck my hair behind my ear and clutch my hands behind my back. "So, please don't kill the messenger, but Franny told me something I think you need to be aware of. It's just speculation. It might not even be the truth. In fact, it probably isn't."

"Breathe, princess."

I take a deep breath and let it out. "Right."

"What's got you all worked up?"

I look around to make sure we're alone and take a step closer to him. "It's about your parents. Someone told Franny the accident might not have been an accident and that your mother was having an affair with Charlie Roberts."

He stares at me silently with his jaw clenched.

Okay, he's not yelling at me yet, but I wish he would say something.

"Who?"

"Who what?"

"Who said it?"

I cringe. Franny asked me to keep Mrs. Roberts out of this. I understand why. The woman is elderly. Franny's worried about her health and how opening up old wounds might affect her.

"I'm not at liberty to divulge that part. This person is confident about the affair but is only speculating about it might not being an accident. I debated about even telling you because it might not be true—the accident part, anyway. I don't want to dredge up anything or cause problems, but I would want to know if it were my family, so that's why I'm telling you."

His jaw shifts like he's grinding his teeth. *Crap!* Did I make a mistake? Should I have kept my mouth shut?

"So you're telling me someone is making accusations about my parents, but you won't tell me who?"

Why didn't I think of that? Of course he wants to know who. What the heck am I supposed to do now? If I tell him, I break my word to my sister. If I don't, then he's going to be rightfully pissed at me.

I cover my face with my hands. The universe sucks. Clearly, I didn't think this through.

A truck door slams and an engine revs.

I drop my hands. Bobby is in his truck and he's leaving.

My mouth drops open as he drives away.

∾

MY PHONE RINGS with Franny's ringtone, and I pull it out of my back pocket. Maybe I should've waited and had her go with me to tell Bobby about his parents. I doubt she would've screwed it up this badly.

"Hey, sis." I stare at the ripples of waves lapping at the boat ramp. A pile of discarded fishing line blows across the ramp. A dragonfly hovers over the water.

"Where are you?"

"Standing at the boat ramp. I just told Bobby about his parents and he is not happy. He took off without a word."

"Yeah, he just did the same to me."

"What do you mean?" I spin away from the lake and walk up the ramp. Did he go to the bakery to get answers?

Of course he did.

"He waltzed into my kitchen and demanded I tell him who told me. He asked how I would feel if someone was spreading vicious rumors about my family." Her heavy sigh echoes through the phone. "Luce, I got all flustered and started stammering. I insisted Mrs. Roberts would never do that. As soon as I inadvertently mentioned her name, he spun around and left. I'm worried. Should I be worried?"

I jog across the parking lot. "Um, well, what exactly are you worried about?" My flip-flops slap against the hot pavement. I could really use my sneakers right now.

"That he's going straight to Mrs. Roberts."

"Yeah, that's a good guess."

"Luce, I can't leave the bakery right now..."

"Don't worry, I'm on my way. I'm already passing by the bakery. Her house is the one across from the inn with the front porch, right? Never mind. I see him. He's walking up her front porch. I'll call you later." I jam my phone in my back pocket after a couple tries as I slow to a walk and try to calm my breaths and heartbeat. I really need to get back to the gym.

I take a deep breath as I turn onto her walk. Bobby and Mrs. Roberts are standing on her front porch. "Hi there." I wave and plaster a big smile on my face.

Bobby looks over his shoulder and scowls at me. "What are you doing here?"

"Franny called when you stormed out of the bakery."

"Why? Does she really believe I'd harm an old lady?" He turns back to Mrs. Roberts. "No offense."

She waves a hand and hobbles over to one of the wooden rocking chairs lining the porch. "None taken. At my age, I'm hard to offend. Why don't you two have a seat. Lucinda, it's nice to see you. Franny talks about you all the time. You're a good sister to her."

I climb the stairs and slip past Bobby and take a seat next to her. Maybe my heart will stop trying to leap out of my chest. "She's a better one to me." Sweat trickles down the back of my neck. Running a few blocks in July heat will never become a favorite pastime for me.

"I'm guessing all this hoopla is because Franny told you about my husband and your mother?"

Bobby folds his arms over his chest and nods. "I'd like to hear the full story from you."

Mrs. Roberts nods her head and stares forward as she rocks slowly in her chair. "My husband was not a good man. He was more than just a philanderer. He was a thief. I supplied the authorities with evidence to put him away, but he was a charming con artist and got himself a shortened sentence." She glances at Bobby and me. "He showed up at my door once again. Thankfully, I don't think he ever found out that I was responsible for getting him caught. He went right back to his cheating, thieving ways." She folds her hands in her lap and looks at

Bobby. "One of his mistresses was your mother. I have emails they sent to each other as proof if you need to see them."

Bobby rests his shoulder against the pole by the stairs. He nods. "An affair is one thing, but what makes you think the boat accident wasn't an accident?"

"I don't have proof of that. If I did, I'd like to believe I might've come forward. I knew what Charlie was capable of and the coincidence of the accident happening shortly after I sent anonymous letters letting all his mistresses see the kind of man he was seems a little farfetched to me."

"You sent letters?"

Bobby's gruff voice makes me want to hug him, but I doubt he would welcome any attempted comfort from me.

Mrs. Roberts nods. "I'm not proud of it. I was hoping people would see him for what he was and maybe I was hoping it would shame those women for messing around with another woman's husband. I never considered he'd die because of it. Or that your father would be harmed. That shame is my cross to bear."

I take her hand. "Mrs. Roberts, you're not to blame for your husband's actions or anyone else's."

"Lucinda's right. Whatever happened isn't your fault for sending some letters. Thank you for telling me." Bobby turns and jogs down the steps and walk to his truck parked in the driveway.

He's leaving without a word—again.

CHAPTER 15

"Tina, your daughter is the most beautiful baby I've ever seen." I stare down at the perfect skin, pert little nose, and blond eyelashes. A tiny fist bats against the pink blanket.

Tina smiles. "She is pretty perfect, isn't she?"

I grin at her and look back down at the precious bundle in my arms. She's so light. It's hard to wrap my head around the fact that this tiny human grew inside Tina and came out so perfect and beautiful.

"How are you feeling?" I glance over at Tina sitting in the glider.

She lifts her hand and drops it. "Oh, you know, exhausted, but ridiculously happy. She hardly fusses at all. She's so quiet that I start to worry and have to check on her every few minutes. The doctor, Ron, and my entire family all assure me she's fine and to enjoy it while it lasts."

Franny peeks over my shoulder and whispers, "Is it my turn yet?" She hands Tina the tea she made her and sits next to me on the couch.

"I suppose. If you really must." I gently transfer Lily to Franny's arms.

"Hello, Lily. I'm so happy to meet you." Franny smiles down at Lily who sleeps peacefully in her arms.

Franny and I drew the short straws and are the last to visit. We didn't want to overwhelm baby Lily or Tina, so the book club ladies all took turns greeting the recent addition and her mama.

Tina yawns and sips her tea.

"Are we keeping you from a nap? Don't they always say to sleep when the baby sleeps, so you get your rest?"

Tina smiles and shakes her head. "They do say that and I'm sure I'll appreciate the advice in the coming months, but right now, I have Ron, Hope, my parents, Jen, and Carter all helping me. Next week, Ron's parents will be here too. Plus, all of you have already volunteered to babysit when I'm ready, and you've all brought over meals so we don't even have to worry about cooking. I couldn't be more blessed."

"We'll have to come up with a schedule so we can take turns helping you and seeing little Lily."

Franny chuckles. "That's my sister, the list maker."

"You and Ron should compare notes, Lucinda. He's got lists going for everything." Tina lets out another yawn.

I grin. "A man after my own heart."

"Speaking of..." Tina smiles.

Ron walks in the room. "Were you speaking about me?"

"Yes, Lucinda likes lists too, and I was telling her you two should compare notes."

Ron winks at me. "Lists are the tools of an organized mind, right, Lucinda?"

"Exactly." I chuckle and peer over at Lily. "She's absolutely beautiful, Ron."

"She takes after her mother." Ron leans down and kisses Tina on her head.

Tina yawns again.

"Okay, we really need to let you take a nap." I stand and walk over to give Tina a hug. "I'm so happy for you."

Ron takes Lily from Franny as we say our goodbyes.

Franny rests her head against mine as we step outside. "Lily makes me wonder about moving up the baby timeline."

"There's a timeline?"

"Mitch and I have talked about it a lot. We planned to wait another year or two, but gosh, my ovaries really jumped to attention holding Lily."

I laugh. "It's hard not to think about having a baby when you hold such a precious angel in your arms."

"Oh, are your ovaries kicking in to gear too?"

"I'd like a baby someday, but I'm rather traditional and would like a husband first. Or, at least, a steady, committed man who I'd like to share my life with."

"It'll happen, Luce." She holds my arm as we walk to our cars. "I can just picture our kids playing together."

I give her a hug. "I want that too. Now get home to that handsome husband of yours."

She waves as she climbs into her car. Her in-laws are visiting, and I have to head back into town to meet with Rebecca about wedding flowers.

Babies. I'll be thirty in less than two months. A month and a half, really. It's August already. I only have a month and a couple of weeks left before I enter the next decade, which means the clock is ticking. Women still have babies in their forties, but the risks go up, don't they? That means if I want to go the traditional route, I need to find a man and settle down in the next few years.

No pressure.

I can see it now: I'll be one of those women who goes on dates and starts asking about commitment and children before we have our first meal because they're afraid to waste any more time.

Ugh. No, I refuse. I can be the happy single aunt who spoils Franny's children. Or maybe having a baby on my own wouldn't be so bad. It's not like I have to decide today.

A car pulls out in front of me and I stomp on the brakes. *Hello! Can you not see me?*

I glance at the driveway the car pulled out of. There's a for sale sign next to a mailbox that has seen better days. An old metal fence leans against a stone wall on either side of the driveway. A large stone house looms over an overgrown yard.

That's some house. I turn in the driveway. What harm can it do to take a peek? It's for sale and the gate is open. Of course, I doubt that gate actually closes anymore. If the stone wall wasn't there to hold it up, it would probably be on the ground.

The driveway circles around a small island in front of the house. There's a wide set of steps leading to the front door. I inch my car past the towering bushes touching the second-story windows over to the portico on the left side of the house. It connects the main house to another building perpendicular to the house. The way the driveway curves around the building, it's probably the garage—a big one.

I stop in front of the portico and gaze through at a sloping lawn with an extraordinary view of the lake and mountains beyond. *Wow!*

This would make an incredible wedding venue. The house needs a little TLC, but brides would kill for that view as they walk down the aisle or celebrate their wedding. The pictures alone would be spectacular. Add in some gardens and it would be perfect.

Granite Cove could use another events venue. Especially if it also had a place for the bride and groom and maybe even the wedding party to stay the night of the wedding. The inn and the two bed and breakfasts are the only places to stay in town. It's only ten minutes outside of town.

What am I doing? It's not like I can afford to buy this place, renovate it, and turn it into an event venue and inn. Nor do I have the experience or time to run an inn while I'm still building my wedding planning business. It would be perfect, though, for someone else.

I glance at the clock on my dash. I'm going to be late for my appointment with Rebecca. I look over at the house one more time. It wouldn't hurt to look it up online when I get home. There's no harm in looking.

"SORRY I'M LATE." I shoot Rebecca an apologetic smile as I walk across her store. She's behind the counter with a pile of flowers in front of her. Her sister stands in front of the counter. Rebecca snips the end of a stem off. Her sleeveless dress skims over her curves.

She glances at the clock on the wall. "It's only a few minutes. Just let me finish up this bouquet and I'll meet you at the table."

I head for the silver metal table on the right hand of the store while smiling at Rachelle leaning against the counter. "Hi. I haven't seen you in a while. How've you been?"

She shrugs and smiles. "Same old, same old. How about you?"

"Busy, thankfully. Wedding season is still going strong."

"I can finish that, Becks." Rachelle walks around the counter. Her cutoff shorts and tank top show off her lean body. She probably wouldn't be huffing and puffing after a jog from the parking lot. I wipe the perspiration off the back of my neck with a tissue. She probably wouldn't be sweating either.

Rebecca pulls out the chair across from me. "What have we got today? I hear the Sanderson wedding was a hit."

It was a small intimate wedding at White Birch Inn last weekend. They would've loved the view from that house. The groom had wanted mountains, and the bride wanted the lake. It would've been perfect. "It was. Your flowers were gorgeous. I heard more than one guest rave about those tall bouquets on either side of the wedding arch."

"I was pleased with how they came out."

"I have a bride who's having a fall wedding, and she wants pumpkins and gourds with flowers. I was wondering if we could actually use some as vases."

"Sure. We could do table centerpieces. We can also do a display with fall colors and pumpkins and gourds. Maybe for pictures?"

I point my index finger at Rebecca. "Exactly. It's a smaller wedding, only about fifty people. Can you put together a proposal for the couple and their families? There's a lot of opinions involved in this wedding."

Rebecca laughs. "Aren't there always?"

I shrug. "Some more than others."

The bell over the front door rings. Rebecca looks up and I glance over my shoulder.

"Jackie, when did you get back into town?" I get up and give her a hug.

"There's an open house at my parent's this weekend so I decided to add some flowers. I'm hoping it will help get their house sold. I was going to call you and see if you were free for dinner while I'm here."

"Absolutely. Have you met Rebecca? Blossoms is her shop. And that's her sister, Rachelle."

Jackie waves to both of them. "Hi. Nice to meet you both."

"Jackie and I have been friends forever. She's trying to get her parents' house sold since they made the move to Florida year-round."

"You're another local then." Rebecca shakes Jackie's hand.

"Born and raised. Though Boston is home these days. What about you two?"

"I've been here a few years. My sister moved here last year."

"Rebecca married Ian Flannigan. You remember the Flannigan brothers?"

Jackie fans herself. "I'll spare you the details of my high school fantasies about them."

Rebecca laughs. "They are a handsome bunch."

"Are they all happily married? Wait, don't tell me. It'll ruin any fantasies that might drift into my dreams tonight."

"Fortunately for your dreams, Ian is the only one married."

"Maybe I need to visit Granite Cove more often." Jackie points to the bouquet Rachelle is wrapping in paper. "I'll take that or one like it if that's for someone else."

"All yours." Rachelle finishes wrapping the flowers and sets it next to the register. "There are more pre-made bouquets, or I can make one for you."

Rebecca smiles. "Rach, are you sure I can't hire you back? I pay more than Joe's Pizzeria."

"I'm happy to help when you need it, but I need to find something for me. Joe's is only temporary."

Jackie follows Rachelle over to the bouquets. I turn back to Rebecca. "I saw this gorgeous old house for sale on my way here that would be perfect for weddings and other events. It has a sweeping view of the mountains and lake. That's why I was late. I got caught up in the fantasy."

Rebecca raises her eyebrows. "Are you looking to buy a place to host weddings?"

"No. I mean I wasn't, but if I had the money, experience, and time, this place would be perfect as an inn and event venue. I could run my business straight from there, and when brides and grooms met with me to plan their wedding, they couldn't help but fall in love with the perfect location. It'd be a win-win."

Jackie puts her hand on the table next to me. "Granite Cove

sure could use another inn. I checked into booking a room for a couple nights while I was here, so I didn't have to worry about keeping the house clean for the open house." She rolls her eyes at me. "You know I'm a slob. Everything is booked solid. There weren't even any rentals available."

I point to her. "Exactly, that's what I mean. It would be perfect. Here." I open my tablet and search for the house. When it pops up with a frontal view of the stone house, I turn it so they can see. I swipe the screen and a panoramic view from the house fills the screen. I suck in a breath. "Isn't it gorgeous?"

Rebecca appears over my shoulder. I swipe through the interior and exterior pictures. There are only four. Besides the front shot of the house and the view, there's only one of a large room with French doors showcasing the view and another of a decent-sized kitchen in need of updating.

"How many rooms does it have?" Rebecca reaches down and swipes up to the details of the listing.

Six bedrooms and a garage apartment.

"Have you seen the inside?" Jackie frowns at my tablet.

"No, I just happened upon it today and drove in to take a peek."

"I'd be interested in looking."

I swing my head up and stare at Rachelle. A look for what? She wants to buy it, or does she just want to see it?

"What are you thinking, Rach?" Rebecca folds her hands on the table.

"I've worked in plenty of hotels and pondered having a B&B someday. I even applied at the White Birch Inn, but they weren't hiring." She glances at me. "I'd like to look. I can't swing the asking price all on my own, but I have some savings. Are you looking for a partner?"

My mouth opens and closes. I look back at the picture of the house. "You're serious?"

"I could handle the inn side while you do your venue side."

I check out the price. It would be steep even with a partner. Then there are the renovations that are probably needed.

Jackie takes the tablet from my hand and scrolls through the listing. "We should make an appointment. Before we make any decisions, we have to see the place in its entirety, make a list of what it needs, how much everything is going to cost, and check out the other inns and venues in the area to see how much they charge so we can accurately forecast revenue."

"We?"

Jackie looks up from the tablet. "I've been looking for an investment. A third partner might make this affordable, don't you think?"

"Sounds like you need to make a phone call, Lucinda." Rebecca slides my phone closer to me.

"Holy crap! It does, doesn't it?" I find the real estate agent's name and number and dial before any of us comes to our senses and changes our minds. It can't hurt to look, right?

CHAPTER 16

"*A*re we crazy?" I give the side-eye to Jackie and Rachelle standing on either side of me.

"We have done nothing but look yet." Jackie plants her hands on her hips and uses her chin to point to the view in front of us. "But I could stand here all day and stare at the view. Get me a chair and it would be even better."

A carpet of green covers the mountains. The evergreen trees would tower above us if we stood close, but I can't help imagining rolling down them like a child on a small, grassy hill. The lake, although miles away, looks ready for us to dive off the hill and into its depths. Islands are scattered across the surface like tiny pockets of color against the deep blue and gray of the water.

"Those five bedrooms upstairs all have their own baths attached. It's like the house was made to be an inn. The downstairs bedroom and bath would be perfect for me. I'd be on site to run the inn and attend to the guests. The bedrooms and baths only need surface renovations, like paint and some fixtures." Rachelle folds her arms over her waist. "We could put a small check-in desk in that nook in the entryway."

Holy crap! Rachelle sounds like she's in. She's right about the bedrooms. Once we get rid of the peeling wallpaper and old carpeting and update the lighting, the rooms will be beautiful. The bathrooms are all a decent size. We might even be able to save the tile in a couple of them. Guests will probably covet the two claw-foot tubs if we can have them refinished.

I tap the toe of my shoe on a square of blue-gray stone. "This big bluestone patio is perfect for smaller gatherings. We could set up a tent over there for larger ones. Maybe add a gazebo, or no, a pergola with flowering vines. Add some soft lighting by adding string lights. Make different conversation areas scattered throughout the grounds, like a fire pit surrounded by Adirondack chairs."

Jackie sighs. "It may look like it only needs surface updates, but we don't know what hides behind the walls. I'm no cook, but the kitchen will need updating for you to offer any meals to guests or for caterers for the events."

"Actually, those are Viking appliances. They tend to last a long time. I could easily provide breakfast, maybe picnic lunches, afternoon snacks to start. We could always expand in the future. Caterers generally bring everything prepared." Rachelle shrugs. "We'd have to have it inspected, of course. Then we'll see exactly what we're dealing with."

Jackie rubs her bottom lip and wrinkles her nose. She used to do that whenever we took a test in school. "We don't even know if we can get the proper permits. This is a residential area."

"Actually I checked yesterday after I talked to the realtor. It's already zoned for commercial and residential use. We can have an inn here, and I can turn one of those bays in the garage into my office. I confirmed it with the town office." I made a lot of calls yesterday after scheduling the walkthrough for today. "I have projections for both the inn and venues as well on my laptop in the car."

Jackie's lips twitch. "You already drew up a business plan, didn't you?"

I lift my shoulder. "Well, there are still details to work out."

Jackie turns to me, folds her arms, and taps her fingers on her bicep. "Convince me."

I could tell her how the great room could easily hold tables and chairs for fifty people. Seventy if needed. The dining room and library can be converted for events to hold twenty-five. When we're not hosting events, they'll be great spaces for inn guests. We can expand the wide gravel parking area in front of the garage for parking without too much expense. Speaking of the garage, we could use two bays to store event paraphernalia between events. And the two-bedroom apartment above it with a small balcony facing the view would be perfect as a bridal suite—or for me. I could live there and then Franny could rent out the bakery apartment for what it's really worth.

None of that would sway Jackie, though.

I lift my chin and throw back my shoulders like I used to do when facing a judge. "According to my calculations, all of which I have reports for, we should clear a profit by year two—eighteen months, if we're lucky."

Jackie narrows her eyes.

Rachelle chuckles. "For what it's worth, I'm in. In case that wasn't already clear."

I clap my hands together and shoot her a grin. We both turn back to Jackie.

Kathy, the realtor, steps out of the house onto the patio. Her high heels and short skirt are a matching canary yellow. Her fuchsia-colored top plasters to her curvy form in the wind. She is not afraid of color. Or snakes. She didn't bat an eye when a long black one slithered across the driveway earlier. Jackie and I both squealed and lurched back. Rachelle kept walking with no hesitation or comment. "Okay ladies, I got my hands on the inspection report from the previous deal on the house." She winks at us. "Don't ask how."

"Why did the deal fall through?"

I glance at Jackie and back to Kathy.

"Not because there's anything majorly wrong with the house, I assure you. The previous buyers had to back out when the sale of their house fell through." She turns a tablet to face us. "You look it over yourselves, but other than aging appliances, it's pretty good. The roof was replaced ten years ago, so you're safe there. The furnace is getting up there, so that might be a concern in a few years. Other than any cosmetic changes you want to make, you're in decent shape."

Jackie scrolls through the document, then hands it to me. "How motivated are the sellers?"

Kathy smiles and cocks her hip. "Let's just say they'll consider any offer."

Driveway lights don't work. There's a dripping faucet in one of the upstairs bathrooms. The aging appliances were already mentioned. The inspector noted we might consider replacing the hot water heater with a higher capacity model. We'd have to update the insulation.

A swarm of butterflies invades my stomach. Is it a swarm? Or is it called something else? I take a breath and hand the tablet to Rachelle. If the inspection is accurate, the renovation costs should be less than my estimation. This could work.

Rachelle hands the tablet back to Kathy and raises her eyebrows at me. I struggle to keep my face from giving away my excitement in front of Kathy.

Jackie holds out her hand to Kathy. "Thank you. We need to talk and run some numbers, but you'll have our offer by the end of the day."

I shoot Kathy a wobbly smile as I shake her hand and then swirl around to stare at the view and so she won't see my eyes bug out of my head or my lips pressed together to contain the squeal of delight.

"Fantastic, ladies. I'll lock up the house. Feel free to enjoy the view a little longer."

Rachelle bumps her shoulder with mine and stares up at the blue sky overhead filled with white puffy clouds. There's a wide grin plastered on her face.

Jackie steps in front of us, facing us, and scans our faces. "The two of you would be terrible poker players." She glances behind us. A car door shutting echoes from the front of the house. "She's gone."

I give a little jump and let loose the squeal I've been holding in. Rachelle dances around in a circle. Jackie rolls her eyes and then shakes her hips and struts her arms like she's doing some kind of combination sixties and nineties dance moves.

We wrap our arms around each other in a circle and grin.

"We're really doing this?" Bubbles of happiness fill me and I giggle. "I can't believe it!"

Jackie steps back from the circle and shakes her head. "They haven't accepted our offer yet. Hell, we haven't even made the offer yet. Don't get too excited."

Rachelle laughs out loud as she throws her arms out wide. "Think positively. This will all be ours." She waggles a finger in Jackie's direction. "At least we know which one of us will be the rational one and reign us in when our dreams out-pace our wallets."

Jackie gives a decisive nod. "That is correct. One of us has to be the hard ass. And as the financial planner, that's my job. You two will be in charge of the day to day." She points at Rachelle. "The inn portion." Then me. "The events." She grins and shakes her hips again. "Feels good though already, doesn't it?"

Rachelle puts a hand over her stomach. "I don't know about you two, but my belly is alternating between a kaleidoscope of butterflies and hunger pains. Why don't we go get lunch and iron out the details?"

Kaleidoscope? That's a pretty image and I guess accurate too.

As we walk to our cars, Jackie looks over her shoulder at the house and then over at us. "Between the comps Kathy gave us, the ones I scanned last night, and the fact that it's been on the market a while, I'm thinking we can offer one hundred thousand under asking."

Rachelle stops by her car. "That's not too low?"

"What's the worst that can happen? They say no with no counteroffer? Jackie is right. I checked out comps too. It's a good starting point."

"Okay, but we need to agree on how high we're willing to go." Rachelle opens her door and waits for Jackie and me both to nod before climbing in.

Jackie and I get in my car and follow Rachelle down the driveway.

Jackie elbows my arm. "Can you believe we're going into business together, just like we talked about in high school?"

I frown and tilt my head. *We did?*

Oh my God! An image pops into my head of Jackie and me in my bedroom sitting on the floor with fashion magazines spread out around us. "That was middle school, actually. We were going to have our own magazine and clothing line."

Jackie laughs. "I'd forgotten that one. Remember when we were freshman? We wanted to open a café on a beach somewhere."

"Oh, Lord. Why did we ever come up with that one? Neither one of us could cook worth a damn. It's still not one of my strengths."

"Me neither, but I think the beach and handsome surfers were our chief inspiration for that one."

"That makes more sense." I reach over and squeeze Jackie's

hand. "I'm so glad we've reconnected. I've missed you." I didn't realize how much.

"Me too."

"I'm trying not to get too excited, but I really believe this is going to work."

"Oh, I have total confidence it is. Lucinda Dawson doesn't fail at anything."

"Tell that to my mother."

"No thanks. That woman has always terrified me."

I start to say me too, but that's not true—at least not anymore. She's done her worst to me and I survived. I even told her off. If I was still speaking to her, I'm sure she would have plenty of negative things to say about my new venture. But I'm not and I don't care what she thinks. This is going to be good for me.

Good for us.

CHAPTER 17

*T*here's a hard knock at my front door. I drop the notebook with my house renovation and design idea on my coffee table and frown at the door. Please tell me it's not another bakery customer wandering up here looking for additional seating. Even though there's a gate at the bottom of my stairs with a sign, which clearly marks this space as private, I've already had two since the patio opened. Once I get my seating on my deck, I'm afraid I'll come out to find customers using it.

How can people not bother to read signs or blatantly disregard them? I still scan over the signs on every door before I enter a store, even if I was in the store recently. Mark used to annoyingly call me his little rule follower. Rules exist for a reason. Without them, society devolves into chaos and people do what they want without regard to other's property.

I swing open the door, ready to *politely* explain what private means.

Bobby stands there. "Hey."

"Hi."

The corner of his mouth lifts in a semblance of a smile, which doesn't reflect in his eyes.

I step back. "Come in."

What is he doing here? I haven't seen or heard from him since he stormed off Mrs. Roberts' front porch the other day.

He walks past me and I get a hint of freshly cut grass. He's dressed in shorts and a T-shirt. He could've come from work.

"How are you doing?"

He rubs the back of his neck. "I need to talk to someone about all this shit, and you're the only one, besides Franny, who knows so..." He shrugs and glances at me standing by the door.

"Of course. Bobby, you can talk to me any time. We're friends, right?" I'd like to believe he no longer considers me any less. "Would you like something to drink?"

He shakes his head. "No thanks."

I point to the living area. "Have a seat."

He sits in the armchair and lifts his chin toward all the papers strewn across the table. "What's this?"

"Oh, um, Jackie and I are going into business together. Rebecca Flannigan's sister, Rachelle, too. Have you met her?"

"Works at Joe's?"

"Yes. We put an offer on a house we plan to turn into an inn and host events there like weddings." I sit on the corner of the couch closest to him.

His gaze scans over the papers. Other than Franny, he's the first person I've told about it. Will he think it's stupid?

"This is the place on Morgan Hill Road, isn't it?"

"Yes. You know it?"

"Yeah, it's got a killer view. I bet you'll have brides and guests lining up for a chance to stay there or have their wedding there."

"That's our hope. I'd actually love to get your thoughts on the landscaping some time if the sellers accept our offer."

"Sure, happy to. When do you expect to hear?"

"We put a bid in yesterday and the sellers countered so we countered, and now we're waiting to see if they'll take it." We're still seventy-five thousand under asking so we still have wiggle

room, but the less we have to pay the more we'll have for renovations.

"Good luck."

"Thanks, but you didn't come here to talk about me."

He rubs his palms over his thighs. "I searched through the
attic. Actually, I went through the entire house, but most of the
stuff from that period of time that has to do with Peyton is in
the attic."

He thinks of her as Peyton and not his mother? I guess it
makes sense since she abandoned him.

"There were a handful of pictures of the three of them
together at parties and on the boat." He stands and wanders
around the room. "One of them was of Peyton and Charlie
looking real cozy in the back of the boat. I don't remember him.
That's not strange; I stayed with my grandparents a lot when
my parents went out."

Bobby grips the back of his neck and continues to pace.
"Nothing I found proves his death was any more than what the
police ruled it—an accident. It doesn't even prove they were
having an affair. The emails could be fake."

"You read them?"

He glances at me and then stares at the floor. "Yeah. Not one
of the highlights of my life. Reading my mother tell some guy
how much she loves and needs him made me sick to my
stomach."

"According to my mother, my father cheated on her. I would
never have believed it if someone else told me. I'm still having a
tough time coming to terms with it. I want to confront my
father about it, but I also want to pretend she never told me." I
scoot back on the couch and tuck my legs underneath me.

"That's the thing. I want to talk to Pops about all this, but
what if he had no clue she was cheating, or it's not true and I
dredge all this shit up for him?" He plops back into the chair

next to me. "It won't bring Roberts back from the dead or Pops out of the wheelchair. Isn't it selfish of me to dig into this just because I want to know the truth?"

"I'm not sure I can answer that for you. I can play devil's advocate and say you're right, it's not going to bring Charlie Roberts back to life or heal your father, but what if it was murder? Then a murderer walks free. What if your father knew about the affair?"

"Pops isn't capable of murder. Get that notion right out of your head."

"I'm not saying he is. I can't imagine it either, but people can do horrible things in the heat of the moment." What would he say if I told him for a few seconds, I considered murdering Mark and his mistress? "Also, did you consider Charlie Roberts was fooling around with a bunch of women? One of them or one of their spouses could've tried to retaliate. Your father was injured in the accident. It doesn't rule him out, but combined with his personality, I'm inclined to lean towards another explanation."

"Is it wrong I believe my mother is capable of murder? I just couldn't come up with a reason, but you just said it. Mrs. Roberts sent those letters to let all his mistresses so they would find out about each other. After reading those emails, my mother would've been the scorned lover. She disappeared soon after the accident."

"Do you want to pursue this knowing your mother could be responsible and go to prison?"

He raises his head and stares at me. "In a heartbeat."

"Then you have to talk to your father and find out what, if anything, he knows and remembers."

"Would you do it if you were in my place?"

"Considering I'm not on the best of terms with my mother right now, I'm not sure I'm the one to ask. I keep telling myself I haven't confronted my father about his affair because he's still recovering from his heart attack, but that's only part of it."

"I'm not on good terms with Peyton either. The circumstances are different, but you can relate enough to tell me the truth."

Would I? I sigh and scrape my nail on the arm of the couch.

"I'm a rule follower and a lawyer. It would nag at me. I'd have to uncover the truth, and I would want justice to be served."

As messed up as my mother is, do I believe she's capable of murder? Under the right circumstances, yes.

Would I turn her in? I really don't know.

Bobby stares up at the ceiling. "I could use that drink now. You have any beer?"

"Actually, I do. Mitch and Franny brought some over when we celebrated the opening of the patio and my finished deck. It's still in the fridge." I grab him a bottle from the fridge. "So, what do you plan to do?"

"I guess I'm going to talk to Pops." He opens the beer and takes a long sip. "Any chance you'll be there when I do? Feel free to say no if it's too out of line."

"If you want me to, I will. Will George be uncomfortable? It's a sensitive topic."

"He really likes you and keeps asking when you're coming back for a visit. He'd be calmer with you there. You tend to diffuse situations and figure out how to make everyone more civil—calmer."

"Thanks." That was a compliment, wasn't it? "When do you want to talk to him?"

"You busy tonight? I'd like to get it over with. We can pick up take-out and head over there."

"I can do that." *Crap, I thought I'd have more time to come up with a way to ease George into the conversation.* Although there really isn't any way to ease someone into a conversation about adultery and murder. "We should pick up some treats from the bakery too. What's George's favorite?"

"I don't think desserts are going to make this any easier, but sure."

Desserts make everything easier. At least temporarily.

CHAPTER 18

"*Y*our father isn't the saint you think he is. Pay me what I'm owed or I'll tell everyone what really happened on that boat." Peyton's voice echoes through the truck cab.

Bobby's hands grip the steering wheel so tightly his knuckles turn white. He stabs at the button to stop the phone connection to his truck. He makes a U-turn.

"What are you doing?"

"Taking you home."

"What about talking to your father? Did that voicemail make you change your mind?" It would've escalated the urgency for me. Obviously, his mother isn't going away.

"No, but I shouldn't involve you in any of this. I'll talk to Pops alone." He pulls over next to the bakery.

"I'm not getting out of this truck."

"Lucinda..."

"No. I'm not leaving you to handle this on your own. That's not what friends do. I'll sit quietly if that's what you want, but I'm going with you."

"Get out of the truck."

I shake my head and grip my hands together in my lap. He's perfectly capable of dragging me out of the truck, but I doubt it will come to that.

"She's gotta be lying, but I don't want to put you in harm's way. She's obviously desperate."

He clenches his jaw, and he's gripping the steering wheel so hard the muscles in his biceps stand out sharply.

I reach over and place my hand on his arm. "Bobby, let me be here for you." No one should face this alone.

He sighs and puts the truck in gear. "I'm not paying her a damn dime no matter what she says. You sure you want to be connected to me if the shit hits the fan?"

"I understand what it's like to be alone when your world feels like it's falling apart. When I quit my job rather dramatically and ended my marriage all on the same day, not one of my so-called friends showed up for me. Not a single one."

"Then they weren't your friends."

"Exactly, but I believed they were. Since moving back to Granite Cove, I've made real friends, and I have no doubt that they would be there for me in a heartbeat. They have been there for me repeatedly. Real friends show up—even when you don't ask them to."

He takes my hand and entwines our fingers. "Thank you."

"You're welcome. Don't delete that voicemail. Blackmail is a crime, and she just incriminated herself."

"They can use it as evidence?"

"Yup. You should bring it to the police so they can document it and you'll have a chain of evidence. Of course, you risk them reopening the boat accident to see if there was any foul play."

"I want to hear what Pops has to say before I do anything else."

He holds my hand for the rest of the drive. When he pulls into his driveway and parks, he stares at his house.

There's an old swing set in the backyard. Did he play there

when he was a kid? I can picture the little blond-haired boy he used to be on the swings. "What can I do for you?"

"Just be here with me." He opens his door and climbs out of the truck. He waits for me at the front while I do the same.

I loop my arm around his and hold his arm with both hands. I'm not sure how to comfort him. His mind must be racing. How would I feel in his place? Probably terrified. I can't even talk to my father over his cheating. It's hard to confront a parent.

As we enter the house, George wheels into the kitchen with a smile. The linoleum squeaks beneath the wheels of his chair. His smile widens when he spots me. "Lucinda, what a surprise. Are you joining us for dinner?" He frowns. "You texted you were picking something up."

Bobby rubs a hand over his face. "I forgot."

"That's okay. I'm sure we can whip something up."

"Pops, we need to talk first."

George's gaze darts between me and his son. "Is everything okay?"

Bobby jerks his chin towards the living room. "Let's go in there."

I perch on the edge of the striped couch. George parks his chair on my left and Bobby stands in front of the brick fireplace. I smooth the material of my sundress to the tip of my knees and clasp my hands together.

Bobby stares at the brown carpeted floor then lifts his gaze to his father. "Peyton showed up in town. She wanted money, and I said no."

George grips the arms of his chair as he stares at Bobby. There's a slight tremble to his bottom lip. Out of fear? Or maybe it's because he still loves his wife and hasn't seen or heard from her in years.

"She came to the house? When?"

"A couple weeks back."

"Why didn't you tell me?"

"Because I didn't want you to have to deal with her."

George wipes at the perspiration above his lip. "You shouldn't have to either. I'm the father. I'm supposed to be the one protecting you, not the other way around."

I pat George's hand. "He did it out of love."

He smiles at me and pats my hand in return. "I realize that." He looks at Bobby. "Is that all?"

"I figured that was the end of it, but she contacted me again and is making threats."

George scowls. "What threats?"

"What really happened on that boat?" Bobby stuffs his hands in his front pockets and watches his father. "I've heard things, Pops. I need to know the truth so that when Peyton comes at me, I'm not reacting blindly. She's threatening to go public."

George snaps his head up. "Public with what?"

"That's what I need you to tell me. What happened? What does she think she knows?"

George shakes his head and wipes the side of his hand across his forehead. "There was a letter in the mail. I don't know who it was from. It said Peyton was having an affair with Charlie." He glances up at Bobby. "I'm sorry, son. There are things I never wanted you to learn."

"She abandoned us, Pops. It's not like I can think much less of her."

George nods. "It wasn't the first time. She'd been unfaithful before. But this time…well, I…it was different." His hand shakes as he lowers it into his lap. "Between that letter and the life insurance…" He closes his eyes and shakes his head.

"What life insurance?"

George glances up and away. "I found out she had increased the policy on me by a lot. I was confused. I went on that boat with them because I needed to find out the truth. I guess I hoped there was a chance it could all be a misunderstanding. I figured on the boat they couldn't just brush it off and walk away. Charlie had a way of talking himself out of anything, and that's exactly what he tried to do. Peyton got angry. Screamed at me. She didn't even attempt to deny the affair. Told me how she needed a real man."

He drops his face into his hands and his shoulders shake. A sob sounds.

I scoot to the edge of the cushion and stare up at Bobby. He's pale as he stares at his father. What should I do? Should I go comfort Bobby or George? I place my hand on George's shoulder. They both need this over. I hand George the Kleenex box from the table. "George, what happened?"

He wipes his face as he raises his head. Tears course down his cheeks. "I punched him. He fell and hit his head. Peyton started hitting me and screaming." He looks over at Bobby. "I never touched her. I tried to cover my head from her blows. Charlie was moaning on the floor of the boat. I kept backing away from her." He hangs his head. "The next thing I remember I was in the hospital. Charlie was dead. I was paralyzed. Your mother emptied our accounts and left."

Bobby drops onto the couch next to me. "What about the insurance?"

George blows his nose and frowns. "What do you mean? The insurance was if I died."

"No, what did she say when you confronted her about the insurance?"

"I never did. I only got as far as the affair. There was the explosion and then she was gone. I just wanted to forget, and I didn't handle everything well after the accident. If it wasn't for you and your grandparents, I'm not sure I would still be here."

I glance at Bobby. He's glaring at the floor.

Had Peyton planned to kill George for the life insurance money? Had she and Charlie planned it together? Then what went wrong? And if that's the case, then why would she risk dragging it all up again?

Unless she doesn't believe Bobby would let any rumors get out to protect his father or even talk to his father about what really happened. Is that what she's counting on?

If George never confronted her about the life insurance, she might believe he never found out. Or it could've been only an accident like the police ruled. A lot of coincidences though.

She could be trying to spin the accident as if George planned it because of the affair.

I scoot closer to Bobby and rub his back. "She probably believes you'll just pay to keep it quiet. She doesn't realize your father, and now you, knows about the insurance. Maybe that's your angle to scare her enough to disappear for good. Unless you decide you want to take all of this to the police and let them untangle it?"

"You believe she was responsible for the boat exploding? You think she planned to kill me and run off with Charlie?"

I angle my head to face George. "There's a lot of unanswered questions. The police ruled it an accident, but they didn't have all the information. It's awfully coincidental."

He grows pale. "Son, I'll do whatever you think is best. If you want me to go to the police and tell them about the affair, the fight, the insurance, all of it, I will. I should have done it back then. I was a coward. I didn't want anyone to know. I never wanted *you* to know. I swear to you the only thing I'm guilty of is being a fool and a coward."

Bobby crouches in front of his father and puts his hand on his knee. "You're not either of those things, Pops. I'm not sure if she planned it or not, but I don't doubt she's capable of it. I'll take care of her, don't worry."

"Stop trying to protect me. What are you going to do? Don't give her a cent."

"I'm not going to. I'm only going to clarify that if she doesn't disappear again and stays gone this time, then I'm going to take it all to the police myself. The affair. The insurance. The blackmail attempt. Everything."

CHAPTER 19

"We never got to have that dinner the other night."

I smile and gaze at my phone on the coffee table. "True. I don't think any of us had an appetite after all the emotion. How is George?"

Bobby's sigh is clear over the speaker. "Good, I think. He's returned to his jovial self. I was worried it might send him back into the depression he had after the accident, but he seems to have moved past it all."

"They say confession is good for the soul. Keeping secrets weighs on a person. He's probably relieved to have it all in the open. Well, at least with you. It's you he cares about. How are you doing with it all? Have you heard from her?"

"Not a peep."

His call to her had been brief. He told her he wasn't giving her any money, that if she persisted, he was telling the police everything. He'd said he bet they'd find the life insurance and blackmail demands really interesting. She'd hung up without a word.

"Good."

"So, how do you feel about pizza?"

"Very fondly."

He chuckles. "Good. I'll see in about a half hour."

"I'll be here."

I collect the papers for the Morris wedding and put them back in my binder for upcoming weddings. I look over the stack of binders and boxes filling the corner of the apartment. I can't wait to have an actual office. I grin and place the binder on the shelf. It's one step closer to becoming a reality. The sellers accepted the offer today. Jackie, Rachelle, and I danced around Blossoms while Rebecca laughed her head off. Now we just have to make it through inspection, appraisal, and financing. One step at a time.

After straightening the remainder of the paperwork strewn across the table, I glance down at my leggings and T-shirt. Should I change? Freshen my makeup? I'm only wearing eye makeup today.

Nope, Bobby won't care, and I've turned over a new leaf. No more worrying about how I look or trying to portray an image that's not me.

I set the two-person bar with plates, napkins, and glasses. I still have a couple of those beers left. Otherwise, it's seltzer or tap water.

The knock on the door comes much quicker than I expected. I glance at the clock on the microwave as I go to the door. It's only been twenty-four minutes.

Bobby grins when I open the door and presents a large pizza box from Joe's. "Dinner is here."

I chuckle and step back. "You made good time."

"For once Joe's wasn't packed. Probably because it's still early."

We each get our slices and settle onto the stools. "So I have some exciting news. I'm trying not to blab to the world about it yet because I don't want to jinx it or anything. They accepted our offer on the house."

"That's fantastic! Congratulations." Bobby gives me a one-armed hug.

I nestle against his warm shoulder for a moment. He's recently showered and shaved. The scent of soap lingers. There's a warming in my core as I take a deep breath.

"We're pretty excited."

"So, what's the plan? You said you're turning it into an inn and hosting events there?"

"Yes. Rachelle is going to run the inn. She'll move into the downstairs bedroom after the closing. We have some renovations to do. I'm turning part of the garage into my office and storage for the event stock. Then there are updates to the rooms upstairs and the rest of the house. I plan to move into the garage apartment so I'm on site and saving on rent. Jackie still plans to stay in Boston, but she'll use my second bedroom anytime she's in town."

"Is Franny aware you're moving out?"

I nod. "She's really excited for us. Of course, she'll be able to charge a lot more rent than I was paying. She insisted on a generous family discount for me. I've felt guilty about that for a while."

"I'm sure you would've done the same for her."

"Yes, but…" I shrug.

"I get it. You don't like feeling beholden to anyone, even your sister." He gets up and gets another slice.

I shake my head when he offers me another one. Two's my limit tonight.

The deck creaks and we both glance over our shoulders at the door.

"Expecting someone?"

"No, but some bakery customers have wandered up here despite the sign saying it's private." I glance at the clock. "The bakery is closed though."

There's a knock on the door and I slide off my stool and answer it.

"Hey babe." Mark leans forward to kiss me.

I turn my head and his lips brush over my ear instead of my lips. *What the hell is he doing here?* I thought I'd successfully avoided him the last time he came to town and made it clear I wasn't interested.

"What are you doing here, Mark?"

"I came to see my favorite girl. We didn't get a chance to catch up last time, so I made another trip." His gaze wanders over me and he chuckles. "Is money so tight you can't take care of yourself, babe? Come back to me. I'll take you shopping and to the spa."

I glare at his smiling face and perfectly styled hair. His polo shirt and shorts are pressed. A waft of cologne wrinkles my nose. What did I ever see in him?

Bobby slides an arm around my waist and rests his other arm on the door. "You ever think of calling first? Because *my* favorite girl is busy."

I wrap my arm around his waist and smile up at him. He's perpetuating the fake boyfriend routine? *Thank God!*

Bobby leans down and kisses me.

His soft lips linger and caress my own. I stretch higher and press my lips against his. My thoughts splinter.

"The gardener boyfriend, right?"

I suck in a breath and scowl at Mark.

Bobby simply lifts a brow. "The cheating ex, right?"

Mark gives him a derisive scan. There's a look in his eyes I recognize. Mark is very competitive, and he sees Bobby as the competition.

Instead of getting rid of my ex by pretending to have a boyfriend, I probably just made him even more interested. Not in me, of course, but in the chase and competition.

I roll my eyes and growl, "Go away, Mark. There's nothing for you here. There hasn't been in a long time."

"I don't think she can be clearer than that." Bobby slams the door in Mark's face.

I slap my hand over my mouth and laugh.

Footsteps retreat across the deck. Is he giving up? For good, I hope.

Bobby smiles down at me. "Think he got the message?"

"Hard to tell. I'm shocked he showed up here the first time. Our marriage ended two years ago. Actually, it ended long before that. I'm not even sure why I married him in the first place."

"Why did you?"

I shrug and fold my arms over my waist. "I think I believed the lie. That we were the perfect couple. I don't think I saw who he really was until after we were married." We both put on a show for each other and everyone else. I never showed him who I really was either. "The cheating wasn't what ended our marriage. He'd done it before. He'd even done it before the wedding, and I still married him."

"So what ended it? Why did you stay?"

"I stayed to keep up the image I had created in my head of the perfect couple, perfect marriage, perfect life. Then one day, it was like a switch flipped in my brain. I didn't recognize myself. I didn't like her much either. I couldn't do it anymore."

"My grandparents are the only couple I can think of who were close to perfect, but even they had to work at it. No one is perfect so how can a relationship be?"

"Wise words."

He smirks. "I have them occasionally."

My fake relationship with Bobby is in many ways more real than my marriage ever was. He sees and accepts me for who I am. I don't feel like I have to put on a show or try to be perfect with him. Mark never would've been there for me when Dad had a heart attack. He would've made excuses and said there was nothing he could do, anyway. Bobby and I weren't even really friends then, but he was there.

He clears the plates. Manual labor and the gym have given him a drool-worthy body. His blond hair curls against his tan neck and over his ears. I bet if it grew out, it would be even curlier.

I toss the napkins in the garbage while I sneak peeks at him washing his hands at the sink. His bottom lip is fuller than his top. There's a very slight bend in his nose. Had it been broken in the past or was he just born that way? His brown gaze lands on me, and a flicker of heat flares in my core.

"Don't freak out on me, okay?"

One blond eyebrow lifts and he leans against the counter. "Okay."

I take a step forward. "What would you say if I said I'm wondering what it would be like if our fake boyfriend-girl-friend relationship wasn't so fake?"

"I'd say I've been wondering the same thing." He puts his hands on my hips and tugs me forward.

My breasts brush his chest. I peer up at him and smile. "You have, huh?" I loop my arms around his neck. "And did you come up with any answers?"

"Just one." His lips capture mine, and I melt against him.

CHAPTER 20

"*H*ey, Jackie. I love your outfit." The colorful print on her romper is cheerful and flattering. I shut my apartment door behind her and follow her over to the couch.

"Thanks. The material is light and comfortable in this heat."

I sit on the armchair and pull my knees into my chest and wrap my arms around my legs. "I was hoping I'd have time to talk to you today before Rachelle arrives." I nibble on my lip.

"Everything okay? You're not changing your mind about the property, are you? Because we already signed the contract and the closing is in thirty days."

"No, no, it's not about the house. It's about Bobby."

"Oh, I thought you two were friends now. Is he still giving you a hard time? I told him the truth about that stuff in high school."

"No, that's all fine. In fact, we're kind of seeing each other." As in daily for the past three days. "I want to make sure you're okay with it." I probably should've talked to her before I kissed him.

Jackie frowns and then laughs. "Why wouldn't I be?"

"Well, you did used to date him. I wasn't sure how you'd feel about me dating him now. I don't want to do anything to hurt our friendship."

"Lucinda, that was high school and a long time ago. We grabbed a bite together when I was in town a few weeks ago. Did I have a momentary thought of what it would be like to hook up with him again? Yes. Was there the slightest spark between us? No. He's an old friend, nothing more."

I curl my legs underneath me and let out a sigh. "Good, because I really like him."

Jackie grins. "I can totally see you two together. You're like the Barbie and Ken of Granite Cove."

I prop my chin on my hand and scowl at her. "I'm not sure Bobby would care for the analogy. I know I don't."

"You're both blonde and gorgeous. I doubt I'm the only one to contemplate it." She winks at me. "Thanks for caring enough to tell me about him."

I reach over and squeeze her hand. "I don't want to jeopardize our friendship ever again."

"Me either. So, give me the juicy details."

"Other than some heavy-duty kissing, there aren't any. It's only been a few days."

"You haven't slept with him yet?" Jackie stares at me with wide eyes.

"Is that weird? Like I said, it's only been a few days. I'm not sure I'm ready to jump in bed with him."

"Well then, you shouldn't. I tend to rush things. Don't use me as an example."

"Can I ask you something rather personal?"

"Of course."

"Do you enjoy sex?"

Jackie raises and lowers her eyebrows comically. I shouldn't have asked her. Obviously, it's a weird and too personal question.

"Your question leads me to wonder if you don't." Jackie draws her legs up onto the couch and turns to face me fully.

I shrug. "I don't think I'm any good at it." I pluck at my leggings bunched under my folded knee. "Mark cheated a lot. A part of me has always wondered if I had been better at sex..."

"Bullshit! Stop that right now. Mark's cheating had nothing to do with you. It's all about him, his ego, and the need for conquest. Don't take responsibility for his failings."

"Logically, I agree with you. But if I'm being completely honest, sex has never been something I felt like raving about or anything. It was okay, but I could take or leave it. It's probably why I've gone the last few years without it just fine."

"Then your partners were selfish asshats. Which, we've already established, they were."

True, all three of them weren't exactly generous human beings to begin with. Ugh, why did I date ego-driven men who only looked good but had no substance? "I guess I had a type, didn't I?"

"You mean egotistical, entitled asshats? At least they were hot."

"Good looks only go so far."

"Which is why they're okay for a one-night stand only. Well, if they never got you off, then they weren't even good for that."

I laugh. "But what if it is me and I'm the one who sucks at sex?"

"Lucinda, the best sex is when it's mutual. Your partner needs to care about your needs as much as his own. Trust me when I say this, Bobby will. You know he was my first, and he was really sweet and caring about it. In fact, I highly recommend having sex with him. Because unless he's completely changed in the past decade, you will enjoy sex with him. He's not the slightest bit selfish."

Okay, on one hand, I hate the image of them together that

just popped into my head, and on the other, I'm feeling rather warm imagining Bobby naked and in my bed.

There's a knock on my door and Jackie hops up. "I'll get it." She leans down as she passes me. "Trust him. He's one of the good ones."

Rachelle strolls in carrying a bottle of champagne. "Sorry I'm late, but I stopped to pick up this." She waves the bottle. "We haven't properly celebrated. I know things can still go wrong." She points to Jackie. "But the contract is signed. The inspection is done. Our financing is done." She looks at both of us. "Any objections?"

Jackie grabs the bottle. "I'll buy the next bottle at closing. Lucinda, where are your glasses? Never mind, your kitchen is so small I'll find them."

"Ha. Ha. They're to the right of the sink."

"Your new kitchen won't be small." Rachelle settles onto the couch and glances over her shoulder at my kitchen. "It's easily four times the size of that one."

"True. Unfortunately, I'm not much of a cook. It might be wasted on me."

"I'll feed you at the inn then. Speaking of which, we need to come up with a name for the inn."

Jackie brings over three glasses and sets them on the table. There's a pop as she opens the bottle and pours. We all take a glass and hold them up.

"To the beginning of a new business venture with three amazing women." Jackie clinks glasses and we all take a sip.

"I've been considering names, too. Why don't we keep it simple and call it The Granite Cove Inn? It would make it come up better in the online searches when people are looking for a place to stay."

Jackie tilts her glass toward me. "Excellent suggestion. I can agree with that."

Rachelle takes a sip of champagne. "That's a good point. I

was toying with names that include the view, but your idea makes better business sense."

Jackie chuckles and pours another glass. "Well, that was easy and painless. If all our decisions are like this, we'll have it made."

"I hate to be the first to burst that bubble, but we need to discuss the renovations budget and schedule. If we want to open before the end of the year, I think we need to prioritize the inn bedrooms and public areas." Rachelle crosses her legs and tugs on her cutoff shorts.

"I agree with that. I can have my office in the apartment. I'm mostly concerned with having a place to meet with clients. I think we need to discuss landscaping, though. We need to have it ready for next year's wedding season."

"Why don't you ask Bobby for his input on the landscaping?" Jackie flutters her eyelashes at me.

"I intend to."

"So are you two a thing now? You should know the gossip has started. I heard whispers of it at work last night."

I stare at Rachelle with my mouth open. "We've only been dating a few days."

"And this surprises you? Hello…small town."

I frown at Jackie. "Do you think it'll bother Bobby?"

Jackie rolls her eyes. "He's lived here his whole life. I'm pretty sure he knows what this town is like."

"Good point."

Rachelle shows us sketches she's done of each of the inn bedrooms with color palettes and furniture ideas. I pull out my tablet and show her the Pinterest boards I made.

Jackie leans back on the couch and says, "This is not my area of expertise. I'll go with whatever you two decide."

"I had a thought to call the rooms after romantic couples since we'll be hosting weddings, but when I did a search, most of them end in tragedy rather than happily ever after. Thoughts?" The search was rather depressing. I doubt a bride and groom will want to stay in a room named after a couple who died.

"Good idea, but I see your point, too. I was leaning towards colors and theming the rooms that way." Rachelle taps her bottom lip. "What about naming them after lakes? This is the lakes region."

Jackie grabs her phone. "I like it. Let's do a search." She types into her phone and her eyes widen. "There's a lot of them."

"I like that idea too. Why don't we each make a list of our favorites and then next time we'll choose from there. We can have little signs made to go over each of the bedroom doors."

"Excellent. What else is on our list today?" Jackie flips through her pad of paper. "Oh, we need to choose a contractor. You two okay with me making some calls?"

Rachelle and I both nod.

"We'll need a website with a way to handle reservations." Rachelle clicks her pen. "Either of you have any experience designing a website? It would save us some money."

"Oh, I talked to Olivia about that. She took a class on it and does the bakery's website. She said she'd be happy to help and is confident we'll be able to design one ourselves." Hopefully, her confidence in our abilities isn't undeserved. I need to make a separate one for my wedding planning business.

We go through each item on all our lists without a single argument. Why can't all discussions go so smoothly?

CHAPTER 21

The branches on the bushes need trimming. I walk down the row between the house and the green line of bushes. I know for a fact Dad has tried to hire Bobby back since Mother last fired him. Bobby delivered a polite no each time. Mother finally crossed the line with him, I guess. A little of it might have to do with how she treated me the last time, too.

Dad waves from the table on their patio when I turn the corner. Since Mother and I still aren't speaking, I've met him here for each of my twice weekly visits. I haven't stepped foot in the house. She hasn't passed on any instructions barring me entry, but I'd rather not give her the chance. Thankfully, she usually makes herself scarce and runs errands.

"Hi, Dad." I kiss him on the cheek and sit.

His silver hair barely moves in the breeze off the lake. He's resumed playing golf so his skin is tan. The doctor has lifted most of the restrictions, physically anyway. He's had to accept a major change to his diet.

"How are you, sweetheart? Do you think you can convince

that boyfriend of yours to come back? The new one your mother hired quit. He did a terrible job anyway."

How does he know Bobby and I are dating? Oh wait, he's referring to when we were fake dating.

"I think Mother burned that bridge permanently. She's fired him and insulted him one too many times."

"Your mother is passionate."

"Then why did you cheat on her?"

Dad's face freezes. Did I say that out loud? *Holy crap!*

I shift in my chair and tug on the hem of my dress. This was not the way I planned to have this conversation. I planned for Franny to be here as backup and to have wine. Lots of wine. I peek at the house. Can I dash inside and grab a bottle? Is she in there watching?

"Where did you hear that?" Dad rubs his palms over his pants and gulps his lemonade.

"Mother, when she was lecturing me on taking Mark back after she called him and told him I needed to be rescued."

"Your mother may have crossed the line in her overzealous efforts, but she does it out of love."

"Does she really? Or does she do it because we don't fit into whatever perfect image she wants us to portray?"

His gaze darts to the house. He's probably planning his escape. Dad usually disappears anytime the conversation gets difficult. I never realized that before. He's always left the raising of us girls to Mother.

"Why did you cheat?"

He rubs his forehead like there's a scarlet letter there he's trying to erase. "It was a long time ago, before I retired. I haven't always made the best decisions, but I love your mother and she forgave me."

"Why do you love her?"

"Lucinda, I know things are strained between the two of you right now, but she's still your mother."

I gaze out over the lake. It's an overcast August day, but the heat is high and people are boating all over the lake.

"I don't understand how cheaters can claim to still love their spouses. If you really love someone, how can you betray them? That doesn't seem like love to me. Mark cheated on me repeatedly and every time he swore it was the last. He promised. I stopped believing him. I don't think he even believed his own lies. He was just saying what he thought I wanted to hear."

"I'm sorry, sweetheart. I didn't know the details."

"Does it matter? I should've dumped him after the first time."

A red tinge spreads across his cheekbones. "Your mother threatened to divorce me. It was a wake-up call. I don't have any excuses. I made a mistake. But all that is between your mother and me."

"Fair enough." But can't he see it makes me look at him differently? He's not the man I thought he was.

"It doesn't affect how much I love you and your sister."

The affair would've been before Franny and I graduated high school since he retired during Franny's senior year. Did he even consider how it might affect us? Am I wrong to think he should have?

"I wish your mother hadn't told you, but I understand why she did. Does your sister know?"

"Yes, I don't keep secrets from her."

He nods.

"Why do you think Mother told me?" He can't possibly think she did that out of love.

"To show you forgiveness is possible. That a marriage, a good marriage, doesn't have to end because of a mistake."

"Mark wanted us to have an open marriage. Should I have just accepted that? Should I have given up all my self-respect to keep up appearances? Should I have stayed in a loveless marriage and been miserable for the rest of my life?"

Dad grows pale and slowly shakes his head. "I did not know.

Your mother never told me." He scowls. "I should've tossed that bastard out on his ass when he asked me to marry you. I never thought he was good enough for you, but your mother..."

Yes, my mother. She saw the polished, wealthy family that would give her bragging rights to all her friends. Is that what I saw too? I'd like to believe I was never that shallow.

"Not every marriage is worth saving. You were right to divorce him." He frowns at the table. "I'll talk to your mother. This distance between you two needs to end."

Distance? Is that what he thinks this is? Does he really believe she'll stop interfering in my life, criticizing my decisions, lying to people because she's ashamed of me, and become a loving, supportive mother who accepts my choices about my life?

Hell will have to do more than freeze over. It will have to sprout flowers and have bunnies, kittens, and puppies frolicking about.

CHAPTER 22

"When you said you had something fun for us to do this morning, I never once thought you meant the gym." Who equates fun with exercise?

Bobby chuckles, takes my hand, and tugs me up the stairs to the gym. "Trust me. And afterwards, I'll treat you to something from The Sweet Spot."

Well, that's more appealing. I won't tell him Franny supplies me with more desserts than I know what to do with. As her sister and tenant, I've become one of her favorite test subjects. That's probably one of the main reasons I needed to join the gym in the first place. Not that I've been back in weeks.

Bobby's black tank top leaves his impressive arm muscles on display. His black gym shorts are long and baggy, hiding his leg muscles, but every time he takes a step, the material hugs his butt. A puddle of warmth spreads over me. Going to the gym wasn't such a bad idea.

The woman at the front desk with very short burgundy hair and giant hoop earrings grins when we step in the door. "Hi, Bobby." Her gaze fixes on our entwined hands, and her smile dims.

"Hey, Maddy." After we sign in, Bobby leads me into the main area and straight over to the weights section. "We'll start you on some light weights. It's all about proper form and repetition."

Great. I force a smile at his boyish grin. It might not be too terrible if he's helping me. At least I'll have an excuse to watch him work out. After all, I need to pay attention to the proper way to lift, don't I? How else can I do that if I don't watch him *very* closely?

His hands skim over my arm as he shows me how to bend and lift in a controlled manner. His foot steps between my legs and his thigh brushes against mine. "Widen your stance to hip-width apart." He grasps my hips from behind and his voice tickles my ear. "Tilt your hips and suck in your stomach."

I swallow hard and follow his instructions.

"That's it. Keep going with the bicep curls."

He picks up a much larger weight and lifts it next to me. His muscles bulge and I feel the burn not only in my arms but in my core—and it has nothing to do with my own exercise.

Bobby talks me through a series of exercises, working everything from my triceps to my glutes. His hands-on instruction for each might have prompted me to ask him to repeat his instructions a few times, okay several.

Perspiration dots my body, but I'm not sure it's solely from exercise.

His gaze lingers on me with every move.

He takes the weights from my hands and wipes them as he sets them down. "How do you feel?"

Like I want to skip the bakery and go back to my apartment so I can ravish his gorgeous body.

I step close and whisper in his ear, "How disappointed would you be if I suggested we end this workout and go back to my apartment to continue a different type of workout?"

His hand wraps around my waist and his gaze fixates on my

lips. "Disappointment is on the opposite spectrum of what I'm feeling right now."

"Then let's go." This time I grab his hand and tug him out of the gym, giving Maddy the side-eye as we stroll past.

Our hands stay clasped as we cross the street and walk down the alleyway between the bakery and the sporting goods store. Trepidation and doubt poke at my brain as the minutes tick by. What if I disappoint him? What if I'm disappointed? I've built this moment up in my head over the past couple of weeks. Each time our make-out sessions have practically scorched my furniture and clothing.

I keep my gaze straight ahead as we walk up the stairs. Will all those customers on the patio know what we're about to do?

Bobby runs his hand down my back as I unlock the door. "Okay? You can change your mind if you're not ready."

I stop. "Have you changed your mind?" That would seriously suck.

He snorts. "Not a chance."

"In that case—" I grab a handful of his tank and pull him over the threshold.

He swings the door shut, leans against it, and yanks me into his arms. His lips and tongue delve into mine as I wrap my arms around his neck. His hands press against my lower back, bringing me flush against his body, and I'm left with zero doubt of how ready he is.

I stretch on my tippy toes to get closer and place the friction right where I need it most.

His lips press kisses across my jaw to my ear. "Should we move this into the bedroom?"

I nod and start walking backwards as he keeps his hands and mouth on me.

We slowly move across the living room to the bedroom. Luckily, my apartment is small or I doubt we'd ever make it to the bedroom. We kick off our shoes as we go.

Bobby presses me against the doorframe and lifts my leg over his hip. I gasp into his mouth at the connection.

He tugs my shirt over my head and places a wet trail of kisses across my chest as he cups my breasts. My nipples poke against my sports bra like they are begging to be released from captivity.

His heavy breaths bathe my breast as he frees one and then the other. My breath stutters in my chest as his mouth closes over a nipple.

I close my eyes and clasp his head to me. The sensation is like a combination of weightlessness and bubbly champagne.

Bobby lifts me against him and carries me the last few feet to the bed.

He tosses his tank behind him and then removes my bra and yoga pants, leaving me in nothing but my pink panties.

His gaze ranges over me, igniting flames. "I think pink might be my new favorite color." He places a kiss on the top of my panties. "Tell me what you like." His voice is low and guttural.

"I don't know...I'm not sure."

"Then let's find out." He stares at me like I'm a present he's unwrapping. His warm hands smooth over my skin. His lips follow, leaving a trail of goosebumps in their wake. "You're so damn beautiful. It should almost be a crime. A guy doesn't have a chance against such beauty."

His lips return to mine for a deep kiss that leaves me gasping. He kisses his way down my body while his hands remove my panties, leaving me bare before him.

He places an intimate kiss on my center and my thoughts scatter.

My legs fall open and my eyes close. A tingle starts at my core and radiates outward as my body clenches and pleasure bursts.

I tremble as he removes his shorts and underwear.

He freezes. "Shit. I don't have a condom."

I point to the drawer of my nightstand. "I bought some. Just in case."

He grins. "That's my prepared princess." He grabs the box and tosses it on the bed before kissing me senseless.

The heat and weight of his body cover mine and presses me deeper into the mattress. It's my turn to map out the planes and dips of his magnificent body with my hands. While my fingers learn the length and girth of his erection, Bobby's forehead drops to my shoulder and he groans.

He takes my hand. "Too much of that, and this will be over way too soon." He kisses me and grabs a packet from the box.

My breath catches as I watch him roll on the condom.

Our gazes mesh as he joins us together. I bite my lower lip and he licks it with his tongue before entwining our tongues in a dance that simulates the movements of our bodies.

An orgasm rips through me seconds before his body tenses above mine and he reaches his pleasure.

He cradles my body with his as our breaths even out and a languid peace settles over me. *I guess I don't suck at sex after all.* Having the right partner definitely matters.

CHAPTER 23

"*J*'m going to miss these frequent impromptu visits. When you move out of the apartment, I won't see you as much. And who's going to be my guinea pig for new recipes?" Franny gives a dramatic pout while she rolls out a crust on the marble counter.

The warmth from the ovens battles the overworked air conditioner. My tank dress sticks to my thighs as I swing my legs as I sit on Olivia's desk. "I know, but my scale will send you thank-you notes instead. You have two weeks left to use me as you see fit. Besides, it's not like I'm moving out of town. I'm sure I'll still be here plenty to discuss wedding cakes and other desserts for my clients."

"There is that and you look gorgeous as ever. I'm sure your scale sings every time you step on."

"Ha. More like groans and grumbles in distress." Although, my workouts with Bobby, both in and out of the gym, must burn an obscene number of calories.

"Do what I did and banish that nasty little bugger to the trash can."

"Did you really? I mean, I've thought of chucking it out the window a time or two, but I never follow through."

Franny pauses and gives me a look. "Please don't throw anything out the windows until you move into your new place. I don't want anyone getting hurt and suing me."

"That's the only thing that's stopped me."

"I really threw the scale out, though. I don't need the added stress. I've stopped obsessing over a silly number."

"That's exceedingly mature of you, and I'm proud of you. Maybe I'll conveniently forget the scale when I move."

"You should. I'll dispose of it for you. It's remarkably satisfying tossing it into the dumpster."

Hmm, maybe I should. Hearing the clang of the metal and knowing I'll never have to tiptoe onto the little square dream killer again sounds immensely satisfying.

"How are things going with Bobby? We should have a double date sometime."

I smirk at Franny. "We tried that once, remember?"

"Hilarious. This time, we will be paired up with the right men, and I won't be searching for an escape hatch to open in the floor next to me."

"It's going good." I glance down at the computer and the stack of papers on the desk.

"Just good?"

I shrug and stare at the tips of my ballet shoes. I should find another pair. I've scuffed these beyond redemption. I flick the tips of my nails. My French manicure is looking a little worn.

"Luce."

"What?" I glance up.

She's standing with her hands on her hips. "What's going on?"

"We've been dating a couple of weeks now and everything is great. I just don't know if he feels the same, and I don't want to sound whiny or needy by asking him. I don't even know if we're exclusive, which is driving me crazy. The thought of him having the incredible sex we're having with anyone else makes me want to commit murder." I drop my head back with a sigh and stare at the ceiling. "Why are relationships so damn hard?"

Franny washes her hands at the sink and walks over and gives me a hug. "If you didn't have powerful feelings for him, it wouldn't be, because then you wouldn't care. Are you in love with him?"

"I just told you I don't even know if he's seeing anyone else. It would be incredibly stupid of me to fall in love with him."

"You're not answering the question, which probably is answer enough."

I drop my face into my hands and groan.

"I think about him all the time. I melt when I hear his voice on the phone. He can make me wet with a look. When he touches me, I instantly go up in flames. It's a hundred times worse than a crush. Which, I might add, must've been all I've ever felt for anyone before. Why didn't you warn me? Why does someone willingly do this to themselves?"

"The uncertainty can be terrifying. I was the same way with Mitch, remember? I almost blew it because I was so insecure. But, finding out he returned my love was like a flower blooming inside me. There's nothing to compare it to."

She puts her arm around my shoulder and rests her head against mine. "The way I see it, you have two choices. Go on as you are and wait for Bobby to define your relationship first. Or just ask him if he's seeing other people. It's not like you have to declare your love for him if you're not ready to."

"You're right. I mean, asking if we're exclusive isn't like I'm asking him to get down on one knee or anything. It's an understandable question to ask someone you're having sex with, right? It's not unreasonable to want to know if I'm sharing him with some skank."

"Just warn me if you're going to murder someone. The girls and I will pick up some shovels and help you hide the body."

I laugh. "Can you imagine? I can just picture Jackie directing us how to dig a hole while Rebecca yells at us to dig."

Franny walks over to the oven and pulls out a tray of cinnamon rolls. The scent fills the kitchen and makes me drool a little. "Rebecca would show up with an excavator from somewhere and have it done in minutes."

I point a finger in her direction. "I can totally see that." I sigh loudly. "So, I should ask him. You're right. I know you're right. The wondering is driving me crazy."

"What were you two giggling about back here?" Olivia walks into the kitchen with a sunny smile. Her blonde hair is pulled back into a ponytail and her white sundress has sunflowers sprinkled all over it.

I wince. "Were we loud?"

"No, not at all. I just caught some of the laughter so now I'm curious. What's up?" Her eyes get wide. "Oh, are you dishing about Bobby? Because I've been dying to hear some details." She scoots over and plops down in her chair. "Tell me."

"What exactly do you want to know? Does he have the body of a God underneath those clothes? Yes, absolutely. Does he know exactly how to use it to drive me insane? Definitely."

Olivia glances at Franny. "Is it getting hot in here?"

We all chuckle.

"Franny and I have spotted him going up your stairs a time or two. We both get a little smile on our faces and then get really quiet while our imaginations go to work."

Franny grins. "Remember when he jogged up the stairs and you were practically hanging your head upside down watching him?"

Olivia blushes and glances at me. "In my defense, he has a very fine derriere. Don't tell my husband—who also has a very fine one."

"Believe me, I've watched him myself. Bobby, not Luke. Although…"

Olivia playfully hits my arm. "They grow them handsome around here, don't they?"

CHAPTER 24

*T*here's another spot of white paint on the window trim. At least Rachelle, Jackie, and I were smart enough to try our painting skills in my apartment over the garage before attempting to paint inside the main house. Luckily, we all agreed hiring a professional was a necessary expense. After two days of our valiant efforts, the walls of my apartment were painted, but it screams of amateur painters. The scent of paint lingers in the air even though the windows are all open. Once I get the rest of my things from the old apartment and out of storage set up, most of the mistakes should be hidden behind artwork, furniture, and window coverings.

"This is the last box." Bobby sets it down on the kitchen floor and glances my way. "The ratio of boxes marked kitchen and the ones for the rest of your place seem to be disproportionate. Are we missing some?"

I stare at the three boxes in the middle of the kitchen. The cardboard boxes almost match the beige tile. I need to add some colorful throw rugs. "Nope, that seems about right. I'm not a chef. I don't need a large assortment of appliances or cookware. The basics work for me."

"Explains why you haven't cooked for me, yet." He slips his arms around me, rests his hands on my lower back, and gives me a kiss.

I place my hands on his chest and kiss him back. The soft cloth of his shirt does nothing to hide the hard planes of his chest. "I can manage a few meals fairly well, but if you were looking for someone with Franny's expertise in the kitchen, you'll be very disappointed. I did not inherit my sister's culinary talents."

He nuzzles behind my ear. "You couldn't disappoint me, princess. I'm no gourmet, but I know my way around a kitchen just fine."

"Oh? Does that mean you'll be offering to cook for me?"

"I could pick some groceries up for your inaugural dinner in your new kitchen. What do you think?"

"That sounds like an excellent idea. I'll unpack the kitchen boxes if you wouldn't mind putting my bed together so I have somewhere to sleep tonight."

Bobby grins. "It'll be my first priority. We can have another first after dinner in your new bedroom."

I laugh. "You don't think you'll be too exhausted after helping me move and then cooking dinner?"

"Please, princess, I will never be too exhausted to make love to a beautiful woman."

Any beautiful woman or just me? It's been a few weeks now but I still don't know if we're dating exclusively. Is he seeing other women? Sleeping with them?

It's not like I haven't had guys ask me out recently. Why does it seem like as soon as a woman is dating someone, guys suddenly find her more appealing? I was completely single for over two years and I can count on my fingers the number of guys that asked me out, but now that I'm dating Bobby, the number is almost the same in only a brief period of time.

There was that guy at the post office just a few days ago. He was good looking and charming, but I had no interest. I guess I'm a "one man at a time" kind of woman. The question is, is Bobby?

"What's wrong?"

I glance up from his gray T-shirt covered chest to his face. "What do you mean?"

"Your smile abruptly disappeared, and you started scowling at my chest. Either I have something on me, or something is on your mind." He peers down at his shirt. "Don't see anything so what's bothering you?"

"Are we exclusive?"

He drops his hands from me and steps back. Okay, not a great sign.

"Look, I'm not asking for some declaration or anything." Although, that would be wonderful and make me stop fearing I'm the only one with strong feelings in this relationship. "I only ask because we're sleeping together. I'd like to know if you're dating other women."

If he says he is, is that a deal-breaker for me? My stomach churns. I really don't like the thought of him dating anyone else, but I don't want to give up on this relationship, either.

"I'm not a huge fan of labels. I haven't called anyone my girl-friend for a long time. All my relationships have been casual for the last several years." He rubs the back of his neck. "Are you saying you want to be exclusive? Or are you trying to tell me you're seeing other guys?"

"I'm not seeing anyone else. I'd like to know if we're on the same page."

He drops his hand and nods. "I can agree with that. I haven't been with anyone else since we hooked up."

His answer is a bit underwhelming, but at least I know we're a couple. Why hasn't he had any serious relationships? Is he some kind of player? I've never gotten that impression from Bobby. Sure, I witnessed him flirting before we got involved, but not in the "racking up notches on his bedpost" kind of way.

"Good, I'm glad we got that out of the way." I point to the kitchen. "I'll get to work on the kitchen."

Awkward much? I roll my eyes as I grab the first box. The floor in the bedroom creaks down the hall. We haven't been dating long, and we still have a lot to learn about each other. Do I wish his feelings were as invested as mine? Duh, of course. I hate feeling like the emotional scale is dipping dangerously in my direction.

My mother's advice of telling me never to love someone more than they love you circles in my head. Great wedding day advice, Mother.

"Hey, I need to grab some tools from the truck."

I glance up from cleaning the utensil drawer. "Okay."

He hesitates by the peninsula separating the kitchen from the family room. "We're good, right?"

I sigh. "Yes, I just feel uncomfortable having that conversation. I don't want to appear clingy, but I also didn't want to be thinking we're a couple while you were dating other women."

Bobby smiles and walks into the kitchen. "I'm glad we had the conversation. I'm not too fond of the thought of you dating other guys." He kisses me and wraps his arms around me. "It's just been a while since I was part of a couple. It didn't occur to me to have an official conversation."

"Why is that?"

He chuckles. "You sound like Pops. He's been after me to settle into a relationship." He shrugs. "As I tell him, I've been busy with establishing my business. What I don't tell him is that for a long time, my attention was split pretty evenly between building my business and taking care of him. There wasn't room for a relationship. Plus, it's not easy telling a woman you still live with your father and can't bring her to your place.

That's something Pops and I discussed recently—me getting my own place."

"You're moving out?" That's a major step.

"That's the plan. Pops has help with pretty much everything he can't do on his own. I'll still bring him to his appointments. Since I run my business out of the garage, I'll be there daily. I'll move my office out of the house though and into the garage."

"So you'll be staying in Granite Cove?"

"Yeah, of course."

"Are you looking for a house, apartment, or condo?"

"Not sure yet. It's all in the beginning stages. Not sure I want the work that goes along with owning a house since I'll still be taking care of Pops' house. I'm also not big on having a lot of close neighbors. I'll have to see what's available. I don't want to be too far from Pops in case he needs me."

The inn is only five or seven minutes from his house. But it's not like we're ready to move in together. Six months or a year down the road it might be a possibility. Although, it would be nice sleeping in his arms and waking up to his handsome face every day.

Dial it back, Lucinda. You just became an official couple; moving in together is not the next step. Getting him to fall in love with me is so I'm not alone in this boatload of feelings.

CHAPTER 25

The phone rings, and I groggily reach for my phone on the nightstand. The screen is blank, and that's not my ringtone. I glance over my shoulder.

Bobby sits up, and the sheet falls to his waist. He picks up his phone. "Yeah?"

It's after midnight. We both must have fallen asleep. He's never spent the entire night. Who would call him this late?

"Shit!" He throws the sheet off and jumps out of bed. "Was he conscious?" He tucks the phone between his ear and cheek as he pulls on his jeans.

I sit up with the sheet clutched to my chest. Is it George?

"Thanks, Chris. I'm on my way."

I scramble out of bed, searching for my clothes. "What happened? Who's Chris? Is your father hurt?" I find a bra and panties and tug them on while hopping around the room.

Bobby yanks his T-shirt over his head and sits on the bed to pull on his socks. "Chris is a friend and an EMT in town. Pops is hurt. Someone broke into the house."

"Oh my God!" I pull on shorts and a T-shirt.

"Listen, you don't have to go with me. There's no telling how long I'll be at the hospital."

I pause with my sandals in my hand. "Don't be ridiculous. I'm coming with you. If you don't want to wait a minute for me, you can go on ahead, but I'm going to the hospital."

He walks over to the door and scrubs his hands over his face. "I should've been there."

I rush over and give him a hug. "Bobby, you can't think like that. Let's get all the details."

He hugs me back tightly and lets me go. I follow him across my apartment, hopping from one foot to the other while I slip on my sandals. I grab my purse off the couch.

I glance over at the inn as I climb into Bobby's truck. Rachelle moved in last week. There's a glow of light from her bedroom. Is she still up?

"Did your friend say anything else?"

He shakes his head. "All I know is Pops was hurt in the break-in and is in the ambulance on the way to the hospital."

"Okay. Is there anyone you'd like me to call?"

"No. There's no one, just Pops and me."

I rub his arm. Who would've broken into his house? Granite Cove isn't exactly a hotbed of crime. The local paper has a police section, but it rarely lists more than a graffiti incident or the occasional stolen bike. *Poor George.*

The town is practically empty as we drive down Main Street. There's only one car that passes us going in the opposite direction. The streetlamps cast a glow on the sidewalks and sides of the road. Instead of a stoplight, the traffic lights blink a cautionary yellow as we drive through. I guess there's no reason for people to stop at each intersection in the middle of the night when almost no one is out.

Bobby pulls into the hospital parking lot. I can't help but compare tonight to the day my father had his heart attack. It was day instead of night, and the fear had felt all-consuming. I glance at Bobby's profile as he parks. Is that how he's feeling now?

I take his hand as we walk to the entrance. He was there for me that day. I hope I can reciprocate some of the comfort he gave me.

Bobby goes straight to the emergency room desk. "They brought in George Calvert. I'm his son."

The attendee gives him forms to fill out and tells us to have a seat and wait for the doctor. Bobby looks like he wants to argue, but the woman is already speaking to someone else. He sits in one of the chairs facing the emergency room doors.

I spot a familiar face. I rest my hand on Bobby's shoulder. "I'll be right back."

Barbara sees me hurrying towards her and stops with a smile, which turns into a frown. "Lucinda, what are you doing here?" She scans me from head to toe. "You're not injured, are you?"

"No, it's Bobby's father, George. He was injured in a break-in. Is there anything you can tell us?"

She looks beyond me to Bobby and then to the woman behind the desk. "Give me a few minutes."

"Thank you so much."

I sit next to Bobby. "Barbara is going to see what she can find out."

"Thanks." He fills out the forms.

I stare at the doors Barbara disappeared behind, willing her to reappear with good news. Bobby can't lose his father. He'll blame himself for not being there to protect him. How could this have happened here in Granite Cove?

Barbara walks through the doors and smiles when she spots me staring. She gives me a slight nod and I sigh. She wouldn't smile or nod if it was bad.

"He was just brought in, so they're still evaluating him. He's conscious and responding. He most likely has a concussion from the contusion on his head, so I don't think he'll be going home tonight. There's a police officer talking to him." She looks at Bobby. "I let them both know you were here in the waiting room."

"Thank you, I appreciate it." Bobby nods at her.

She smiles. "My pleasure. I'll do my best to give you updates while you're waiting."

I squeeze her hand in gratitude before she walks away.

"Good news, right?" I smile at Bobby and wrap my arm around his. "He's probably charming the doctors and nurses while we speak."

Bobby gives me a small smile. He finishes filling out the forms and brings them over to the desk.

A police officer walks out of the doors and Bobby strides across the room to meet him. "Anthony, were you on the scene with Pops? What can you tell me?"

The officer pats Bobby's shoulder. "He's good, man. He intercepted someone rifling through your office. I told him to leave the hero stuff to us guys in uniform. We're going to need you to go through everything and report what's missing."

Bobby puts his hands on his hips. "Any idea who it was or what they were looking for?"

Anthony frowns and shakes his head. "George said it was a man he saw, but he thinks someone else hit him from behind. He's fuzzy on the details after that. He dialed nine-one-one before he lost consciousness."

They clasp hands and Anthony slaps Bobby on the shoulder before walking to the exit.

I close the distance and take Bobby's hand.

He glances down at me and pulls me in for a hug. "I'm glad you're here."

"Me too."

∼

"IF YOU WANTED to spend more time with me, all you had to do was ask." George winks at Deirdre, his nurse.

She playfully swats his leg as she walks by. "You have me for five more hours until my shift ends."

Bobby and my gazes meet across the bed. They moved George into a room on a different floor. His slight concussion hasn't stopped him from charming his doctors and nurses.

Deidre types something into the computer outside his door and then walks down the hall with a wave.

George watches the doorway for a moment. "There's something I didn't share with the police."

"Why the hell not?"

"I'm not one-hundred-percent positive, and I wanted to talk to you first because it concerns you."

Bobby leans forward and rests his hand on the side of the bed. "If it could lead to identifying whoever broke in and attacked you, you need to tell the police."

"Even if I heard the man call the other one Pey?"

As in Peyton, Bobby's mother? She's so desperate for money that she'd not only break in but assault George? And who is her accomplice?

Bobby rears his head back. "Especially then." He jumps to his feet. "Damn it, I should have gone to the police the moment she showed up in town, trying to get money out of me."

George sighs. "You're right. I should have told them what I think I heard. He said he was going to stop back in the morning. I'll tell him then."

Bobby drops into the chair. "I'll stop by the station and tell them the rest of it."

I fold my hands in my lap. "I'll go with you. I was a witness to her blackmail attempt."

George looks between Bobby and me. "You both should go home and get some rest."

"Save it." Bobby glances at me. "You can take my truck. There's no reason for you to stay here the rest of the night."

Should I go? The doctor said they would likely release George today. I glance at the clock on the wall. It's a few minutes past three. I'd be able to get a few hours' sleep before my appointment with a bride. I'd planned to reschedule, but she's high-maintenance and probably wouldn't take any change in the schedule well.

"If you're staying, I'm staying." I just wouldn't feel right leaving him here. I'll have to fortify myself with caffeine. I can sleep after the appointment.

George frowns at us both. "There are plenty of medical professionals here to take care of me. I don't need the two of you babysitting me, too." He waves his hands at us like he's brushing us away. "Go."

I stare at Bobby. His eyebrows meet in a frown.

"George might be right. If we're all going to speak to the police in a few hours, we should get some rest."

George nods. "Very sensible, Lucinda."

Bobby scowls at his father but stands. "Fine, but you call me for anything."

"I will."

I kiss George on his cheek. "I'm very glad you're okay."

"I'll take a bump on the head any day if gets me a kiss from a beautiful woman."

I smile and shake my head at him.

Bobby and I walk to the door.

"Oh, wait. I thought of something the other day when I took the ferry ride with Hal and we stopped in Wolfeboro. I meant to tell you, but I keep forgetting. It's probably nothing, but I ran into Charlie once coming out of the bank in Wolfeboro. I thought it was odd at the time. I mean, why wasn't he banking in Granite Cove? Anyway, when I greeted him, he seemed surprised and nervous. He tried to get rid of me, too. Do you think you should mention it to his widow? See if she knew why he did his banking a few towns over? You said he was a crook. It might've been something shady."

What reason would someone choose to drive almost an hour away to go to a different bank? I suppose there could be many innocent reasons, but considering what Mrs. Roberts has shared about her husband, I think it has to be worth checking into if possible.

"As his widow, Mrs. Roberts would be the one most likely to inherit any accounts or have access to a safe deposit box."

George and Bobby both glance at me.

"If he held the account with someone else, then obviously that person would get it. But she should be able to at least ask the bank what type of account and who was on it, if there was an account."

Bobby sighs loudly. "Looks like we'll have a busy morning."

CHAPTER 26

I might need a fourth coffee. I rest my head back against the headrest and close my eyes. Bobby and I got a few hours' sleep before heading to the police station. They appeared to take the threat seriously as they took down both our stories and listened to the voicemail Peyton had left demanding money.

When we parted ways, Bobby kissed me on the forehead and held me for a few minutes outside the police station. I can only imagine what must be going through his head. I had dashed off to my meeting with my high-maintenance bride while Bobby had gone to his house to see the damage they'd done and figure out what they took.

He said other than hurting George and making a mess, it didn't appear anything was missing. What could they have been looking for?

I turn my head to Bobby, driving. "Do you think she could've been after proof of the life insurance you told her you found? That's silly. She'd have to know there are digital copies of everything these days. Destroying one paper copy won't do much if people already know about it. They could just print out another copy."

"You're assuming she's smart enough to figure that out on her own."

Mrs. Roberts taps her cane against the console between the seats. "You don't have a very high opinion of your mother, do you?"

Bobby glances in the rearview mirror at Mrs. Roberts. "Do you?"

She snorts. "Point taken." She gazes out the window with her hands folded in her lap.

She hadn't wanted to come with us, but she had made the call to the bank and found out Charlie had a safe deposit box there. A dig through a pile of keys she'd thrown in a drawer because she didn't know what they went to produced the key. The quickest way to get access is through her as his widow. I understand why she doesn't want to keep reliving her husband's deceit. There could be anything in the box, or nothing at all. He could've emptied it before his death, and because he never closed it, it sat empty in the bank. As long as someone paid the bill, the bank wouldn't do anything. The small account he held there made sure it was paid.

Bobby's fingers flex on the steering wheel. We'd taken my car, and he'd insisted on driving. I was too tired to protest.

The bank is in a nondescript brick building that looks like a dozen other characterless brick buildings you see being built lately. We accompany Mrs. Roberts and wait while she shows her credentials.

We follow the bank employee back to the vault. Once they insert the keys, he holds out the box to her. She points a finger at Bobby, who takes it, and we follow him to the viewing room.

I hold the chair for Mrs. Roberts to sit.

"I don't want to know what's in there. You can do with it whatever you want."

I smile at her. "What if it leads to a million dollars? Just think what you could do with that."

She snorts. "That man never seemed to have two nickels to rub together. He married me for access to my parents' money. I accepted that truth long ago."

I put my hand on her shoulder. Maybe this wasn't such a good idea. She's been through enough. We should've found another way or let the police handle it.

Bobby lifts the lid on the box. It's not empty. He shuffles through some papers. "They look like life insurance policies." He glances sideways at Mrs. Roberts. "One is on you. The other is on my mother."

How would he have taken one out on Peyton? And why?

He holds up a tiny tape. "Anyone own one of those old-fashioned recorders?"

"I do." Mrs. Roberts purses her lip and places both hands over the top of her cane. "The never-do-well might've confessed to all his crimes. He liked to keep souvenirs and news articles reporting his crimes. It's how I found out what kind of man I had married."

Bobby stares at a piece of paper.

I lean forward. "What is it?"

"I think it's a diagram of Pops' boat."

I suck in a harsh breath. "Do you think it's proof he intended to murder your father and he and Peyton would collect on the life insurance?"

Bobby looks at Mrs. Roberts and then at me. "I think he might've planned to make sure he collected on a few policies."

Mrs. Roberts raises her chin. "Don't think you're going to shock me. I used to worry he'd kill me off. Especially when he came back from prison. I was terrified he'd find out I was the one who sent him there."

Good Lord! The stress the poor woman must have been under. How could she have continued living under the same roof as someone she felt might murder her in her sleep? Then again, I guess that might be what victims of abuse endure daily.

"There are more tapes in here and more papers." Bobby looks at Mrs. Roberts. "Do you mind if we take all of this with us? Would you consider letting me give it to the police for the case against my mother?"

"I don't care what you do with any of it. I don't want to know the extent of his crimes. At my age, all I want is peace. The only reason I'm here is because I don't want the guilt of doing nothing on my conscious anymore. That may be selfish of me…" She lifts her fragile shoulders.

I put my hand on her shoulder. "It's not selfish."

"I can understand wanting the past to stay buried. My father and I are both guilty of feeling the same way. Unfortunately, Peyton has made that impossible, and it's time for her to pay for her crimes. I'll limit your involvement as much as possible, but I have a feeling the police will want to speak with you."

"It's fine. For years, I expected the police to show up at my door. I'll tell them what I know. Perhaps then he'll stop haunting my nightmares."

AFTER NEVER SETTING foot in the Granite Cove Police Station my entire life, I've now been here twice in one day. Well, at least the parking lot this second time around. The gray stone blocks of the building resemble those of my inn. It would make sense if they were from the same quarry. The back of the building is an obvious addition, with white siding.

I glance up at the wide stone steps and the double glass doors. Bobby has been in there for over a half hour already. Should I have insisted I go with him, despite his objections? He'd gotten awfully quiet and broody as the day wore on.

It's not like I can blame him. Listening to those tapes must've been brutal for him. Peyton isn't even my mother, and I was horrified. The three tapes of her voice clearly implicated her in planning George's murder. She confessed to forging George's name on the life insurance papers while bragging she forged his name all the time. Mrs. Roberts only agreed to listen enough to one tape to confirm it was Charlie Roberts' voice calling Peyton "Pey Pey" on the tapes. Why would he have made the tapes, let alone kept them? He was careful not to make any confessions, but it's evidence he had knowledge of the crimes. He had clearly been prompting her to implicate herself. Why? Blackmail? Or evidence if she turned on him?

He'd been planning to backstab her. The life insurance policy on her with him as the beneficiary was fairly damning. He probably planned to do away with George and Peyton both in that boating accident, but George kiboshed the plan when he confronted them and knocked Charlie unconscious. With him being dead, we'll probably never know.

It'll probably be difficult for the police to identify the people on the other tapes in the box. I'd only heard bits and pieces of them. Bobby was understandably more focused on the ones with his mother.

Bobby jogs down the steps. His blond hair lifts off his forehead in the breeze. He pins his gaze on the ground in front of him. The navy-blue T-shirt complements his coloring. I should buy him some more clothes in that color, maybe a dress shirt and a polo shirt for dinners out.

I stretch across the car and open the passenger door for him. Hopefully, he won't argue that I switched seats when he went inside. He needs a break. Maybe he'll take the opportunity to rest his eyes and mind for a few minutes.

He climbs in without a word. He's not carrying the bag with the contents of the safe deposit box anymore, so the police must've kept them.

"What did they say?"

"She's now wanted for attempted murder instead of only the assault and breaking and entering. Apparently, it'll make the police more interested in finding her. There's a host of lesser charges too. There's also a warrant out for her arrest in Alabama. Drugs."

He clenches and unclenches his fists on his jean-covered thighs. "They had a tip she and the unidentified male were staying at a trailer park two towns over. But by the time the police got there, they were gone."

"They'll catch her."

He turns his head and pins me with his gaze. "Will they? Or will she keep destroying our lives piece by piece?" He yanks on the seatbelt. "Drop me off at the hospital. Pops is scheduled to be released."

"I'll wait and bring you both home." I start the car.

"That's okay. I had one of my guys drop off Pop's van. It's easier for him."

"Of course. I could still come inside and help."

"No, we're good. He said the paperwork is all set, so it'll only take a few minutes."

I back out of the parking space. "How about if I go to your house and get it cleaned up from the break-in and the police? I could pick something up for dinner on the way. I'm sure George will be hungry and you must be starving." We hadn't eaten since breakfast and it was almost dinner time. My stomach protested more than once while I sat in the parking lot waiting for him.

"Most of the mess is in my office. I'll take care of it later. You should go home and get some rest. It's been a long couple of days. I'll heat something up from the freezer for Pops."

Is he being considerate or just trying to get rid of me?

He seems to have thought of everything. I guess I'm not needed or wanted.

The silence in the car weighs heavily as I drive to the hospital. Maybe he just needs some space to process everything that has happened. I can understand that. It takes me a while to feel all the feelings and think through everything when something traumatic happens in my life.

I pull up to the hospital entrance, and he releases his seatbelt and opens the door. "Thanks—for everything. I'll talk to you later."

"Okay—"

The door slams behind him and he strides through the automatic doors of the hospital.

I blink several times at his retreating back. I can't be mad at his abrupt departure. He's going through a lot. I put the car in gear. A night of rest will do wonders for us both. Who knows, perhaps the police will have arrested Peyton by the time we wake up. Wouldn't that be a pleasant surprise?

CHAPTER 27

$\mathcal{R}$achelle sets down a tray with a pitcher of lemonade, glasses, and sugar cookies. "I thought we could use your client meeting as a little test subject, if that's all right with you. It's fresh squeezed and the cookies have a hint of lavender. They're both recipes I've been tweaking and considering offering once we open."

"Excellent idea, and the tray is adorable." The flowers and old-fashioned tea service are colorful and charming.

"Thanks, I couldn't resist buying it." She looks around at the couch, table, and umbrella set up on the corner of the inn's patio. "This set is very inviting. I think the guests are going to love it."

I spread my hands over the white cushions. "It is fabulous, isn't it? I fell in love with it the second I saw it. Of course I imagined it would go on the deck of the bakery apartment, but now I realize it would've overwhelmed the space. I can't believe Franny bought it for me." I roll my eyes and grin. "Well, I actually can. She's the best." She surprised me, too.

"It's a good thing she wasn't able to cancel it once you announced you were moving. It really works here."

Franny was afraid I'd want something completely different for the inn, but the set fit this side of the patio perfectly.

"I was thinking of asking your sister for some advice on a few potted flowers for the patio. What do you think?"

Rachelle scans the entire patio. "I'm having lunch with her, so I'll ask. It's a great idea."

"I'll pay for them since I'll be using this space for meetings until my office is done. It's not like we'll have any guests until the end of October." I gaze over the hills. "I really hope we have time to take advantage of the leaf peeping season."

"You and Olivia did a fantastic job on the website. When it goes live tomorrow, I'm sure guests will book like crazy." She crosses her fingers. "I hope."

"It's your pictures that are going to get people to want to stay here. They're perfect." How lucky are we Rachelle is a talented amateur photographer? "I was thinking we could even update the header photo of the view from the inn as the seasons change. What do you think?"

"I love it. And once they finish the rooms, we can add those too."

The bedrooms and bathrooms are scheduled to be done the first week of October. The rest of the public areas will be completed by the following week. As long as everything remains on schedule, we can start taking on guests by the third weekend in October.

"What do you think of having a soft opening and having our friends and family stay in the rooms for a night before we officially open? It would be both a celebration and a way to get everyone's opinion and feedback."

I grab Rachelle's arm. "That is an amazing idea! We can have Franny and Mitch, Rebecca and Ian, Olivia and Luke, Kerry and Holden, and Tina and Ron." I tick off the rooms with my fingers. "Perfect."

Rachelle grins. "It'll be fun and hopefully get any kinks out before the paying guests arrive."

"I'll tell Jackie. She can stay in my second bedroom. Oh, I'll have to get a bed for her to sleep in."

The sound of a car driving on the gravel driveway announces the arrival of my client.

Rachelle touches my arm and stands. "I'll leave you to your meeting."

"Enjoy your lunch." I walk across the patio and down the short set of steps to the portico. I had instructed Brooke and her mother to pull underneath the portico and that we would meet outside. They're both easygoing, and so far, they're a delight to deal with, so I knew it wouldn't be a problem that my office isn't finished yet. A few more weeks and it should be.

"Hi!" Brooke exits her car with a giant grin. She gasps. "Oh my God! Look at the view!"

Her mother toddles forward on three-inch heels. "It's gorgeous!"

"Isn't though? It took my breath away when I first saw it. It's what led to me and my partners buying the property and turning it into an inn. You're the first clients to see it."

Brooke turns to me with her finger against her lips. "Are you planning to host weddings here?"

"We are." A saw echoes from inside the house and I chuckle. "Obviously, it's not ready yet. We plan to open the inn portion at the end of October."

She wants her wedding in the fall of next year, but she hasn't chosen a venue yet. I might have had some secret hopes she would consider the inn for her wedding.

Brooke and her mother share a look and her mother gives a slight nod.

"I want it. Will it accommodate sixty people? That's how many we're planning to invite."

I wave my hand toward the French doors. "Yes, the ballroom

can comfortably host seventy. I can't show you right now because they're working in there, but I can show you the pictures of what it'll look like when it's completed. As well as the guest rooms upstairs." I point to the upstairs. "All the suites on this side have Juliet balconies." It might be a stretch calling the great room a ballroom, but it spans the width of the house and it sounds better for a wedding venue.

"How darling." Brooke's mother clasps her hands together.

"Why don't we have a seat?" As we walk across the patio to the couch, I open my hands and gesture to the grounds. "The grounds will all be landscaped, of course. We're planning to add a pergola with flowering vines and conversation areas scattered throughout." We haven't quite finalized those plans yet, but there's plenty of time.

I pour each of us a glass of lemonade and offer them a cookie. Brooke takes a bite and then peers at the cookie. "This is delicious. Is this from The Sweet Spot? I want them to do my cake."

"No, the innkeeper made those. Divine, aren't they?" I haven't actually tried them yet so I take a nibble. They are delicious. They're soft with just enough of a crust not to crumble in your hands and the lavender is so subtle, but it gives the taste an elegant touch. Rachelle could actually give Franny some competition with these cookies. "The Sweet Spot is my number one recommendation for wedding cakes, and not just because my sister, Franny, owns the bakery."

"Does she really? Oh, I simply love going there." Brooke's mother takes another cookie.

Brooke leans closer. "Is it true she married Mitch Atwater?"

"Yes, it is."

Her mother frowns. "Who is he?"

"He's a famous director, Mom." She shakes her head.

"So, here are the mockups of what the inn's interior will

look like when we're finished." I spread the pictures out on the table.

"I love this one." Brooke taps the picture with the white and gold comforter.

"That's actually the one we plan to offer our bride and groom as part of the wedding package." Score one for me.

"It's lovely." Her mother scans the other pictures. "I assume you'll offer a discount for booking all the rooms?"

"Of course." I haven't drawn up a price list for that but I will.

I pull out a copy of the checklist I made for my clients. "This is a list with timelines of everything we need to arrange to make your wedding day exactly what you imagine. I can also email you a digital copy. You can add ideas you find online, and if you choose, it will be shared with me so I can help make it happen. As you see, choosing a venue, a date, and budget are at the top of the list and one of the first items you need to decide on."

How fantastic would it be if they choose The Granite Cove Inn for their wedding and we have our first wedding booked today?

Brooke is practically vibrating in her seat. "I want the first Saturday in October. It's when Tyler and I went on our first date. Is that available?"

"Let me see." I open my tablet even though I know it's available since it'll be our first. Brooke's mother hadn't blinked when I placed the price list next to the checklist. "It's all yours."

Brooke squeals in delight and claps her hands. Her mother has tears in her eyes. Hopefully, they're from joy and not because of how much this wedding will cost.

I pull out a copy of the contract. "This is our contract for hiring me as your wedding planner and this one is for booking The Granite Cove Inn as your venue." I lay the second one down next to the first. "As you can see, I'll need a separate deposit for both, and this is the schedule for the remainder of the payments. I'll send you an invoice if you decide to book all the rooms. This is for the venue and the bridal suite."

I hold my breath as she signs each one. She opens her purse and pulls out her checkbook. "Is a check okay, or do you prefer credit card?"

"Whichever you prefer." I can't wait to tell Rachelle and Jackie. I'm doing a dance on the inside.

They linger over lemonade and cookies. I get Brooke set up on the digital checklist and show her how it works.

I walk them to their car and smile and wave as they drive away. As soon as the gravel stops crunching beneath their tires, I dance across the patio with my arms in the air and a stupid grin on my face.

Out of breath, I plop down on the couch and kick my heels off. These shoes were not meant for dancing on stone. They match my sky-blue dress though.

I pull my phone out of my folder to call Jackie. She's going to be thrilled. She's anxiously waiting for bookings so we have revenue coming in.

When I open my phone, I see a notification: a voicemail from Bobby.

Finally. I haven't spoken to him in two days since I dropped him off at the hospital. I unsilence my phone. It's a good thing I always silence it during meetings, but I wish I hadn't missed his call. I miss his voice.

I press the playback button with a smile.

"Hey, Lucinda, I've been thinking and it's best if we step back from the relationship. I've got too much going on to focus on dating anyone. I hope you understand. Take care of yourself."

I grip my phone in my hand and stare at the screen. Bobby just dumped me—by voicemail.

CHAPTER 28

$\mathcal{I}$f I connect all the marks on the ceiling, I bet it would resemble a constellation or an abstract painting. Where did they all come from? Did previous tenants throw a ball at the ceiling? They could've been tall and placed their dirty fingers all over the place. Why didn't I paint the ceilings when we did the walls?

Oh yeah, we hate painting and we suck at it.

My phone buzzes against my stomach. I glance down at the text from Franny.

I'm worried about you.

Me too.

Rachelle says you haven't left your apartment in days except for a client meeting and...

I tap on the text to read the rest.

to see the finished bridal suite, which she said she had to drag you to. I know you're sad, but you weren't this depressed when you got divorced, Luce. Let me pick you up after work and take you back to my house. I have the next two days off. I'll pamper you. We can eat ice cream and trash men.

I stare at the three dots blinking on the screen.

Has it been days? I turn on my side on the couch and snuggle underneath the blanket.

The bridal suite is beautiful. Any bride who stays there will feel like a princess.

Princess. He who I refuse to think about called me that.

Luce?

Franny means well. She brought a box of all my favorite treats when I called her hiccupping and sobbing. I glance over to the box still sitting on my counter, empty of course. The crumbs will probably attract an army of ants.

She's right. I wasn't this depressed after my divorce. But I didn't know what love was then. I didn't feel it deep in my bones. It was more like a surface attachment.

I text Franny back. *Maybe tomorrow. I'm really tired.*

You can sleep here.

And watch Mitch fawn all over Franny and stare at her like she's the best thing that's ever happened to him? No thanks.

I'm a terrible person.

I love you and I'm sorry, but I just want to be alone right now. Okay?

The three dots appear and disappear.

Okay. I love you. I'm here if you change your mind.

I shut off my phone and drop it on the table.

I just can't deal with anyone's pity and sad eyes. Rachelle showed up with Rebecca the day after with wine. Rebecca offered to slash his tires. Rachelle said she would put sugar in his gas tanks. I made them both promise not to. He doesn't need any more disasters in his life.

Is that what he saw me as, another disaster he had to deal with?

There's a hard knock on my door.

Was Franny texting on her way here?

No, she would never drive and text. She yells at me every time I do even though I dictate the texts instead of typing.

I stare at the door. How bad would it be if I ignored it? They might believe I'm not at home or sleeping.

It's probably Rachelle. Is another of the suites done?

The knock comes again.

I trudge over to the door and open it. I blink hoping the vision before me is a hallucination.

"Good God, did someone die? You look horrible. And these stairs are a death trap. I almost twisted my ankle when my heel caught on a hole." Mother pushes past me and stalks into the apartment.

I've died and gone to hell, haven't I?

"Really Lucinda, it's rather bland. And what is that smell?" She eyes me up and down like it's coming from me.

I suppose it could be. I drop back onto the couch and cover up with the blanket. Maybe if I ignore her, she'll disappear.

Why would she choose now of all days to start speaking to me again? To gloat over my misery?

She waltzes into my kitchen and starts dumping boxes and containers in the trash. She's cleaning now?

"Did you hear they arrested that woman and her accomplice?"

I jerk to a sitting position. They arrested Peyton?

She glares at me from the sink. "You're well rid of having anything to do with that family. Blood always tells."

And there it is. She's here to rub it in my face that she was right about him.

"Mother, Bobby is a good man and so is his father. He's not responsible for what his mother has done. If people blamed everyone for the type of parents they have, then Franny and I probably wouldn't have a single friend."

There's a crash from the kitchen. She stands with her back to me gripping the edge of the counter. Is she contemplating murdering me?

I shrug and scoot into the corner of the couch and pull my feet up.

Do your worst, Mother.

"Your father convinced me to come here."

Did he really? "Why?"

She turns and folds her hands in front of her. Her eggplant-colored blouse and cream-colored slacks are stylish and expensive. There's not a blonde hair out of place. There isn't a frown or twitch on her classically made-up face.

"You might want to ease off on the Botox, Mother. I can't tell if you're angry or trying to appear contrite."

Her eyes narrow. Anger it is.

"This was a mistake. I don't understand where I went so wrong with you."

"How about the constant criticisms? Or the vicious condescension? Maybe it had something to do with you holding us up to some ridiculous standard and making us feel like garbage when we couldn't reach it?"

I flick my nails together as I stare at her angry face. "You know, you've never once apologized for anything. You interfere and justify your actions like it's in our best interests. But it never is. It's only what you want. If Dad sent you, I bet he was under the very misguided perception that you would apologize."

Her gaze drops to the floor. Bingo.

"If you don't make some changes, you're never going to see any grandchildren. Franny and I will be too afraid you'll scar them like you've scarred us."

I walk over to the door and open it. "Goodbye, Mother. Don't come back unless you're ready to apologize and change your behavior. Go to therapy. Own your shit."

She stalks past me. "Vulgarity is beneath you, Lucinda. If I'm so awful, why are you the one alone, *again*?"

I slam the door behind her. Direct hit, Mother—as always.

CHAPTER 29

*B*obby walks out of Blossoms carrying a giant, gorgeous bouquet. I stop dead on the sidewalk. People move around me. He's buying flowers for another woman already? He never bought me flowers.

Rebecca sold him flowers to give to another woman?

She's running a business. I can't be mad at her for it. Can I?

Tears sting at the back of my eyes. How could he move on so quickly? Did I mean nothing?

He reaches his truck and opens the passenger side door. He's wearing a dress shirt and pants. He dressed up for another woman? She must matter to him. Unlike me, who meant less than nothing.

I stalk down the sidewalk in my pink heels.

Bobby spots me as he shuts the door and turns around. His eyes widen and a smile appears. "Hey."

Hey? A smile? He not only dumps me as his girlfriend but as a friend and he acts like nothing happened?

I wrap my arms around my waist wrinkling the pink linen dress I spent a good half hour ironing this morning. "You don't want to be my boyfriend anymore, fine, I'll live." *So what if it sent me into a depression for days?* "The way you did it was cowardly, but whatever. It's rather a moot point when the result is the same. What I don't accept or understand is that we were friends first—at least I thought we were. You don't just cast aside friends like they're worthless. It's rather ironic that you disliked me so much for the way you thought I treated people, but here you are treating me carelessly."

He steps toward me and I back up. He lifts his hands and drops them. "I'm sorry. You're right about all of it."

"I know I am." *Wait, what?*

Tears threaten and my mouth waters. I twist my lips and swallow hard. I will not cry in front of him.

"I was going to come see you."

I roll my eyes. "Sure you were." I jerk my chin to the flowers. "Before or after you delivered those to your new conquest?"

Bobby glances in the truck and frowns.

He didn't think I saw them? That I wouldn't find out from Rebecca? He could've at least had the decency to buy them from somewhere else.

He opens the door and grabs the flowers. "They're for you." He holds them out.

"Do you seriously believe I want someone else's flowers?"

"Read the card."

My gaze drops to the silver and turquoise card with Blossoms logo on it. I pluck the card from the holder. The card could be generic enough he thinks he can pawn them off on me. Would he do that? I hadn't thought so before. Of course, I never thought he'd break up with me over voicemail either.

I glance up at him and flick open the card.

Happy birthday, princess. Please forgive me.

He remembered my birthday is today. Unless he calls every woman princess and it happens to be their birthday too. The odds probably aren't high on that, which means the flowers are for me.

I take a deep breath. The perfume of the flowers is heavenly. I peek at him over the top of the bouquet. "Thank you."

He smiles and my heart flops in my chest. What exactly is he asking forgiveness for? Because I can provide him with a list.

"Do you have plans or can I take you to lunch?"

"Actually, I just had brunch with Franny."

I won't tell him she showed up this morning, dragged me out of bed, and stuffed me in the shower. Then basically dressed me like a child while she lectured me the entire time about not letting an idiot man who was obviously too stupid to see how wonderful I am make me hibernate and wallow in misery. She said some pretty meaningful things about how proud she is of me for confronting our mother and father and starting two businesses from scratch. She's right; in the past, I never would've confronted them. I wouldn't have confronted Bobby either. I would've probably slinked around the corner so he didn't see me.

He nods. "Any chance we can go somewhere and talk? There's some stuff I want to tell you."

"I heard about Peyton and her accomplice being arrested."

"They both should go to prison for a long time."

"Good. You and George must be relieved. Franny said Mrs. Roberts is happy the truth is finally out." She also said Bobby has stopped by to visit her.

"I really am sorry, Lucinda. I handled it badly."

So he's sorry for the way he did it, not for doing it in the first place. I straighten my shoulders and paste a smile on my face. "I appreciate the apology and the flowers. See you around."

I walk past Blossoms down the sidewalk. Crap! I had meant to visit Rebecca, but I'm not exactly in the mood right now. And my car is in the opposite direction so I either have to do an about-face and look like an idiot or loop around the block. I suppose I could dart into a store until he leaves.

This is ridiculous. So what if he sees I went in the wrong direction? A girl is allowed to change her mind. I spin around and almost sandwich my flowers into a very wide chest.

I stare at Bobby's white dress shirt and the V-shaped tan skin visible beneath the open collar. "What are you doing?"

"Following you until I can figure out a way to get you to forgive me."

"Fine, I forgive you for dumping me by voicemail."

"That's a start." He gently lifts my chin.

I drag my gaze up to his.

"I'd really like a chance to explain."

"You look handsome." I wave a hand. "In those clothes."

"Thanks. You look beautiful."

My lips twitch. "Thank you."

"I made that call when I knew you were in a meeting and would've silenced your calls. I knew I couldn't do it in person or even if I heard your voice because I would change my mind."

"I don't understand."

"I was trying to protect you. Pops had already been hurt. We had just confirmed that she was capable of murder. I didn't want you anywhere near any of it. I knew you wouldn't stay away unless I did something drastic."

I lower the bouquet slowly. "You broke up with me to protect me?"

"Yes. Don't you see? Now that they've arrested her, I was coming to explain everything."

I smack him with the flowers. Buds and leaves fly in every direction and their scent fills the air. I smack him again.

"You broke my heart to protect me? I'm not a child, Bobby! I don't need a big strong man to protect me. I need a partner who's going to stand by me and let me stand by him during the good and the bad."

People walk by giving us the side-eye and a wide berth.

He pulls me into his arms and rests his chin on top of my head. "You're right. I'm sorry. I'm an idiot. I was so damn afraid of something happening to you because of me. I couldn't bear it. I love you."

"You've got a funny way of showing it. And I love you too."

He chuckles. "You do?"

I drop what's left of the flowers, wrap my arms around his waist, and snuggle against his chest. "Yeah, I do. That's why it hurt so much."

He cups my cheeks. "I'm so sorry." His lips caress mine in a slow, exploratory kiss.

I close my eyes and breathe in the scent and taste of him. I've missed this. I've missed the feeling of his muscular arms around me.

"You know it's terrible for business to have customers see my flowers used as a weapon." Rebecca stands next to us with one eyebrow raised tapping the toe of her shoe against the sidewalk. "On second thought, I can make some throwaway bouquets and market them that way. If a man, or woman, did you wrong, hit them with flowers. You'll be less likely to be arrested for assault." She swipes the rest of the bouquet off the sidewalk.

I cringe. "Sorry about that, Rebecca."

She laughs. "I'm just kidding. A customer came in the store with a tale about a gorgeous wild woman beating an equally gorgeous man with flowers and I just had to see for myself. Imagine my surprise when I saw it was the two of you." She looks between us. "Judging by the kiss I just witnessed, you two won't be maiming any more flowers?"

I give her as contrite a look as I can manage while happiness is surging through me. "No more maiming your beautiful bouquets. I promise."

She scowls at Bobby. "Then can I assume you've done the groveling you promised me?"

I laugh. "She made you grovel?"

Bobby winks down at me. "She made me demonstrate on my knees."

"Speaking of which, why are you still standing?" Rebecca taps her toe again.

Bobby sighs and starts to lower himself. I grab his arms. "We've made enough of a spectacle of ourselves today. But you can show me the full groveling later in private."

"Deal." He kisses my forehead.

"In that case, happy birthday." Rebecca gives me a hug. "I have a feeling your afternoon and night are now booked, but call me so we can celebrate your birthday."

"I will, thank you."

She points the destroyed flowers at Bobby. "Can I also assume you want me to replace this once beautiful arrangement I spent a great deal of time on for one of my closest friends so she can properly appreciate them for longer than a few minutes?"

"Yes, please."

"I have your credit card information, and I'll add a delivery charge as well."

I pat Bobby on the chest. "You don't have to do that." I was the one who attacked him with them.

"Yes, I do."

"Yes, he does."

They both laugh.

Rebecca winks at me. "Call me."

I smile as she walks away. She would never sell Bobby flowers for another woman. Not while she knew I was hurting so badly. She's a loyal friend.

"Your place or mine? I have some heavy groveling to do. Fair warning, if you pick my place, Pops will be there to add his very strong opinions of what an idiot I've been for letting you go."

"I miss your father."

"And he misses you—vocally and repeatedly."

He pulls me in close and buries his face against my neck. "God, I've missed you."

CHAPTER 30

*H*ammering drags me from sleep. The construction crews must be starting early this morning—unless I slept in. I prop one eye open and glance at the clock on my nightstand. Eight o'clock. It is a little early. I slide my foot back in search of a warm male leg.

I stretch farther and farther but encounter nothing. I turn over. The pillow is indented, but Bobby is gone. Did he leave? I sit up, holding the sheet to my naked chest. It's Sunday. He doesn't have to work. Did he leave in the middle of the night instead of staying over?

The pillow puffs around my head when I drop back. We had a beautiful day yesterday. He actually got on his knees as soon as we walked in my apartment and apologized repeatedly. Then he got on his knees again later in my bedroom and made me forget my own name let alone anything he'd done needing forgiveness.

Why would he leave? I untangle myself from the sheet and grab my robe off the chair. The blue silk slides against my skin. I tie the sash and walk down the hall to the kitchen. There's a coffee and a box from The Sweet Spot on the counter next to the new bouquet delivered yesterday. He went to the bakery, came back, and left again?

The coffee cup is still warm. I take a sip and sigh. I peek into the box and pull out a blueberry muffin. There are a couple of raspberry turnovers in the box. Franny must've forgiven him. She vowed never to make him another one when he broke up with me. She wanted to fire him from being her landscaper too, but I made her promise not to.

He didn't leave a note.

The fresh scent of blueberries fills my nose as I take a bite of the muffin. It's fluffy, sweet, and has a hint of lemon. Perfect.

That hammering seems awfully loud to be coming from inside the house. I wander over to the window and peek outside as I take another sip of coffee.

I blink but the mirage doesn't disappear. Bobby, shirtless, builds something across the yard. What is he doing?

I suck in a breath. Is that a pergola?

I put the coffee and muffin down on the table and dash down to my bedroom. I can't go outside in my robe. The construction workers will arrive any minute. I stop dead outside my bedroom. No they won't—it's Sunday.

I run back to the door, picking my coffee and muffin up on the way. Other than a few winces, I make it down the stairs and across the patio without incident in my bare feet.

Bobby grins at me. "Happy birthday."

I glance at the four posts and the large array of plants and bushes scattered around in pots. "You're building my pergola."

"This is where you said you wanted it, right? I can move it if it's not." He frowns down at the ground. "I should've made sure, but I wanted to surprise you."

"It's perfect. You did all of it this morning? How did you plan all this and get it all here so quickly?"

"I did the planning part weeks ago. And the purchasing of materials."

"You've been planning this for weeks?"

"It's your birthday."

Mark's idea of a birthday present was to tell me to buy myself something nice using the household account. I chuck the rest of my muffin and set the coffee down on the table. I take several gingerly steps across the grass and then leap into his arms. "Thank you."

He laughs as he catches me. "You're welcome. I'll show you the plans for all these plants and you can nix anything you don't like."

"I love them all. I love you."

"I love you too, princess."

"Let's go back inside."

"But I'm not done."

I nibble on his earlobe.

He moves his hands from my thighs to my ass and starts walking.

I chuckle against his neck and kiss my way up to his lips.

Our kiss turns heated. We strain against each other.

He stumbles down the patio stairs but keeps us both upright and our mouths together.

By the time we make it up the stairs and into my apartment, we're both panting.

We never make it past the couch. The need is too strong. Within minutes, we both reach completion.

I stare dazedly up at him. A blond curl is plastered to his forehead. He gives me a boyish grin. "I guess you really like the pergola."

I swat his shoulder.

He chuckles, kisses me, and rolls to the side, pulling me back into his arms.

"Are you still planning on moving out of the house and getting your own place?"

He nods. "Yeah. I haven't started looking though. I didn't want to leave Pops alone with all that stuff going on."

I trace my fingers over his chest. "How would you feel about moving in here—with me?"

I feel his gaze on me. "You want me to move in?"

"It's close to the house so you can still check on George and run your business." Is it too soon? He probably thinks it's too soon.

"You don't have to give me reasons, Lucinda."

I peek up at him smiling down at me. "I don't?"

Bobby sighs and steps back. "You know what Pops said to me in between telling me how stupid I was to let you go? He told me to ponder why you really rubbed me the wrong way for so long."

"What do you mean? Didn't you tell him about Jackie and Sal and my not-so-great high school persona?" I cringe. Will George think less of me?

"Those were just excuses I told myself to avoid the truth." Bobby rubs his bottom lip. "You're gorgeous. You turn heads wherever you go. I was never an exception. It used to piss me off."

"You were attracted to me so you treated me like crap?" Like a playground boy pulling a girl's ponytail or something because he likes her?

"I'm not proud of it, but yeah, that had a lot to do with it. I told myself you were just a pretty package. But seeing you smile or hearing you laugh did something to my gut every time. Then you confronted me on my shit and I lashed out at you for it." He puts his hands on my hips and drops his forehead against mine. "I still feel bad about it. The more time we spent together, the more I realized the genuine beauty was beneath the packaging. You care deeply about everyone. When you love someone, you're all in."

"Thank you. That was sweet and I appreciate it. I totally forgive you. So, does that mean you *do* want to move in?"

He chuckles. "As long as it's what you really want, then my answer is yes."

I grin and slip my arms around his neck. "It's what I want."

He kisses me. "I'm paying rent."

"Are we talking money or landscaping and your other areas of expertise?"

He chuckles. "Those are just side benefits." He kisses my cheek. "I like the thought of having you in my arms every night."

"Me too."

"I'll even take on the cooking."

I slide my leg over his. "This arrangement keeps getting better and better."

EPILOGUE

I drop my tote on the chair inside the door and slip my shoes off. The morning wedding with the afternoon reception on the ferry was supposed to be one of my easier events this wedding season, but running up and down the stairs between decks made my feet and calves sore. It's only the middle of May. I have at least one wedding every week for the next month and a half.

One of our flameless candles is lit on the table with a covered plate in front of it. I glance around the apartment. "Bobby?"

I pick up the folded card in front of the plate. *For my hardworking princess. I knew you wouldn't eat at the reception so I made you something.*

He's right, there wasn't time. I smile and lift the lid. Risotto, my favorite.

Where is he? I touch the plate. It's still warm. He must've just made it. I walk through the apartment calling his name. My phone buzzes in my pocket.

Enjoy your meal. Love you.

Where is he? Maybe he had to run over to see George. I sit

and pick up the wine glass. A light fruity scent wafts up. Another favorite. I text him back. *Thank you. Come home soon.*

The creamy risotto melts in my mouth. I close my eyes and groan. My boyfriend is a hell of a cook. I ordered risotto at a restaurant months ago, and he not only got the recipe from the chef but makes it for me anytime he thinks I need a little comfort food. Like when I've spent the day on a deck of a boat trying to make sure the bride and groom have the wedding day of their dreams.

How lucky am I?

The meal disappears off my plate in a short amount of time. I wipe my mouth on the napkin and swallow the last sip of wine. I stand and lift my plate to carry it to the sink. There's another note under the plate.

You're even more beautiful on the inside than you are on the outside (and that's saying a lot). Pour yourself another glass of wine and come out to the patio.

I glance at the door and smile. What is he up to?

After pouring myself another glass, I slip my feet into my sandals by the door. They're not exactly a coordinated choice with my navy dress. I open the door and peek outside. There's another candle glowing on one of the small tables Rachelle and I added last month on this side of the patio.

That wasn't there when I arrived, was it? I would have noticed.

I scan the landscaped grounds as I walk down the stairs. Bobby created a masterpiece back here and in front. He built the fire pit we envisioned surrounded by white Adirondack chairs and added a circle of lavender to repel mosquitos. Beautiful clematis vines cover the pergola he built. Green spiraled bushes line either side. A row of rocking chairs sit on the long narrow patio he made to match the one attached to the house so people can sit and admire the view. There's a rose garden and a small herb garden on the side for Rachelle to use in her cooking for inn guests.

You've brought me more joy than I knew was possible.

Tears threaten as I drop the note and search the area.

A candle flickers to life across the patio on the table in front of the couch. Are they on a timer? What is he up to? I stride across the stones and pick up the note propped in front of the candle with a single red rose.

Whenever I contemplate the future, you're always in the center of it. I wouldn't want it any other way.

I bury my nose in the fragrant rose and purse my lips together as tears fill my eyes. I put down my glass of wine and wipe a tear off my cheek. Is this a proposal? Dare I hope?

Lights glow all over the pergola twinkling like a hundred fireflies. I gasp. He strung lights on the pergola?

I jog down the steps and over to the entrance. I stop. Flower petals cover the ground.

Bobby is on one knee holding a ring box out.

"I love you, Lucinda. Will you marry me?"

I slap a hand over my mouth as a sob escapes.

"Princess, I really need an answer here. I think my leg fell asleep waiting."

I gasp out a laugh and leap across the space separating us, tackling him to the ground. "Yes!"

He rolls with me in his arms. "Whew, for a second there, you had me worried."

"I love you so much. It's perfect. You're perfect." I plant kisses all over his face.

He pushes my hair back from my face. "You're the one who's perfect—perfect for me."

He kisses me softly. "You up for planning another wedding? Because I can't wait to call you my wife."

"We could elope."

"The wedding planner wants to elope?"

I bite my lip. If we elope, then we'd be married that much sooner. But then I wouldn't have Franny, George, and the rest of our family and friends with us.

"I can plan a wedding practically with my eyes closed. We'll have it here." I gaze up at the purple flowers interspersed with the lights. "Right here. With all our loved ones. Small and intimate. Only a dozen—twenty-five tops. I'll check the schedule. We can have it on a weeknight. A few weeks at most."

Bobby chuckles and kisses my cheek. "Whatever you want, princess."

THANK you for reading *A Change in Perspective*! If you enjoyed the story, please consider leaving a review.

OTHER BOOKS in the Granite Cove series:
My First My Last My Only : Franny's story
Covet thy Neighbor : Olivia's story
No Choice at All : Rebecca's story
Whispers & Broken Promises : Tina's story
A Yearning Dilemma : Kelly's story

TO HEAR ABOUT UPCOMING BOOKS, sales, giveaways, and exclusive excerpts, sign up for my newsletter: http://eepurl.com/dt5N7M

ABOUT THE AUTHOR

Denise Carbo writes Romance and Women's Fiction. She is a voracious reader, loves to travel, and is fascinated by the supernatural.

She lives in a small, picturesque, New England town with her high school sweetheart and their three amazing sons. Find out more at https://www.DeniseCarbo.com and sign up for her newsletter to be the first to hear about new books, sales, giveaways, and exclusive content. https://eepurl.com/dt5N7M

ALSO BY DENISE CARBO

My First My Last My Only

Guilt & Redemption

Bloodlines

www.ingramcontent.com/pod-product-compliance
Lightning Source LLC
Chambersburg PA
CBHW071434260626
47170CB00008B/2710